Jennifer Johnston is recognized as one of Ireland's finest writers. Her other books include *The Captains and the Kings*, *How Many Miles to Babylon?*, *Shadows on our Skin* (which was shortlisted for the Booker Prize in 1977), *The Old Jest* (winner of the 1979 Whitbread Award for Fiction), *The Christmas Tree*, *The Railway Station Man*, *Fool's Sanctuary*, *The Invisible Worm* (which was shortlisted for the Sunday Express Book of the Year in 1991) and *The Illusionist*. *Two Moons*, her first novel for three years, will also be published in Review.

The Gates

Jennifer Johnston

review

First published in Great Britain in 1973
by Hamish Hamilton

First published in this edition in 1998
by REVIEW

An imprint of Headline Book Publishing

10 9 8 7 6 5 4 3 2 1

ISBN 0 7472 5935 6

Typeset by Avon Dataset Ltd, Bidford-on-Avon, Warks

Printed and bound in Great Britain by
Clays Ltd, St Ives plc.

Headline Book Publishing
A division of Hodder Headline PLC
338 Euston Road
London NW1 3BH

For my children

Run In

Cathleen wept her thousand welcomes and farewells. Her cold tears splattered the airport runways, and the quaysides of Dublin, Galway and Belfast. They doused the cows under the Wicklow hedges and the sheep huddling together on the unprotected slopes of the north-west, and the groups of cold men waiting for the pubs to open. Ladies in the glistening streets of Dublin lowered their umbrellas and stepped into the welcoming doorways of lighted shops and tea-rooms. Professional men behind their desks thought, with resignation, of the cancelled racing, and the cold journey home, nose to tail all the way to desirable neo-Georgian houses in Foxrock, Ballybrack and Killiney. Women with cold red arms placed buckets below the larger holes in their roofs, and laid the *Independent* on the surrounding boards. The water splashed tunefully into the galvanized pails. Babies cried. The clouds pressed so low that the hilltops were lost, and only the heaven-pointing steeples of the churches kept the swirling mist off the land itself. The east wind blew ceaselessly, cold as charity.

Chapter One

February 3.
Home at last. Uncle Proinnseas was so cold on the station platform that I couldn't work out whether he was pleased to see me or not. Ivy made up for any chill in his welcome by the warmth of hers. Tears and hugs. Nothing changed in the last five months. I never want to leave.

*   *   *

The train was late. No sign of it at all. Up in the signal box Jimmy was reading the paper, tea steamed by his hand in a large china mug. The Major sighed, and the steam of his breath hung for a moment in front of his face, and then was knocked for six by the wind. He clenched and unclenched his swollen fingers inside his pockets and stamped his feet on the platform. His shoes had the shine of much loved mahogany. Hand-made, Lobbs, always paid in the end to get the best. Look after inanimate objects well and they served you well. His diamond-patterned socks were neatly darned just above the heels. The wind carved its way through his cord trousers and the stretched flesh holding his bones together, even through his army greatcoat, now stripped of its military trimmings, and kept for days when the east wind was at its most painful. It seemed to have grown too big for him over the years, now looked as if it had once belonged to some larger, more confident man. Some hero of the mud and trenches, one of the few to return from Flanders, the Somme, the great pushes, the flower of England's youth. He stamped his foot irritably, a chilblain on his little toe was giving him hell. No distant whistle blew. They wouldn't have him in the next lot. 'Sorry, old chap,' they said at the War Box, looking at him, he felt, with a certain disdain. After that special trip he'd made and all, thrown around on that infernal Mail boat, reeking of vomit and Guinness. The train dark from Holyhead to Euston, London dark. 'Sorry, old chap.' Some pink-faced incompetent, who'd never seen more service than playing bang-bang on Salisbury Plain. And back he had to come, play blasted nursemaid to Bertie's kids, while Bertie cavorted round Africa with the Eighth Army, my field glasses, borrowed, but never returned, round his neck, and a jumble of meaningless ribbons over his pocket. Admired, loved by his men, another Irish general winning England's wars for her. Bloody officialdom. 'Sorry.' And they had the effrontery to take the other, in spite of his Sinn Fein and Communist mumbo jumbo in the newspapers, they took him. Highly likely to put a bomb in one of their letter boxes, blow up Buckingham Palace, but no 'sorry, old chap' there. It would have served them right if he had shown himself in his true colours.

His head and neck poked out tortoise-wise from the khaki shell. His eyes watered and two tiny tears trekked down the furrows in his cheeks, skirting the corners of his grey moustache, and were dried by the wind on his chin. Still no whistle from up the line. Soon the light would be gone. Damn it to hell. Hated those roads in the dark. The lights in the Ford were packing in. Must see Greely about a new battery. Money draining away. Wastepaper basket full of unopened bills. Best place for them. Great little car, though. Must be all of twenty-five years old. Nothing made like that nowadays. Blown together, like everything else. Nothing made to last longer than a year or two. Pouring money into the pockets of the manufacturers. He chewed at the corner of his moustache with decaying teeth and looked hopefully towards the signal box. Jimmy still had the paper in front of his face. No point in standing there in the cold. He turned into the shelter of the hall. It wasn't much warmer and you could smell the gents. Nip out to the car for a minute or two.

'Is it yourself, Major?'

'Ha,' said the Major, stopping in his tracks and looking round.

The station-master, hatless, genial, smiled across the half-door leading to his own private room. Behind him glowed a heaped coal fire.

'Nice to see you, Macken.'

The Major changed direction, and strode, hand outstretched, towards the station-master. For years now, since things had drifted, hard times settling in, he had worn, during the colder parts of the winter, a pair of old brown gloves with the fingers cut out. He still suffered from chilblains though, and his fingers drove him mad at night, flaming and itching, until he longed to rip the discoloured skin off with his nails. The station-master shook the offered hand. The chill from the five fingers penetrated his fat palm.

'You're famished.'

'It's the bloody east wind. It cuts through you. I can't say I'll be sorry when the winter's over.'

The station-master opened his little door and stepped out into the hall. He made a fat bow towards his room.

'Come in and have a warm up. Is it the Dublin train you're waiting for?'

'Minnie.'

'Sure enough. She's fifteen minutes behind time, anyway. You've still a wait ahead of you. It's seldom we see you round these parts. Please avail yourself.'

'Splendid,' said the Major. 'Kindness itself. I'll be with you in a minute. Must just pop out to the-ah-car — see she's ah, yes . . .'

'Quite.'

One of the station-master's eyelids dropped fractionally in spite of himself.

' . . . locked.'

The station-master thought of his own Austin Cambridge gleaming in the garage not a hundred yards away and smiled complacently. You needed your wits about you in this world, and wits weren't something the Major was bursting with, God help him.

'I've a fresh pot of tea just made.'

'Splendid.'

He almost ran out into the street. The Ford was parked about twenty yards down the hill, opposite the Railway Bar. He opened the kerbside door. No eyes peered from curtained windows, no one moved nearby. The lights from the Railway Bar were reflected gaily in the wet road. He leaned over into the back and felt under the rug on the floor. The blood rushed to his head, and for a moment he felt dizzy, thought he was going to faint. His hand gripped hard on the back of the seat. After a moment he straightened up. It was all right. He wiped his mouth with the back of a brown mitten and closed the car door again. He locked it carefully and put the key in his trousers pocket. He walked slowly back to the station, and into Mr Macken's room. The heat was tremendous. Mr Macken had drawn two chairs up to the fire, in anticipation.

'Sit down there now, Major, and get some of the chill out of your bones.'

The Major opened his greatcoat and sat down, feet outstretched towards the blaze. The chilblains began to stir. Mr Macken was pouring stewed tea out of a tin pot.

'Sugar?'

'No thanks. Cosy little place you've got here.'

The station-master handed him his cup.

'My sanctum sanctorum.' He winked. 'You'd be surprised what goes on in here. It's more than just seeing trains through the station, I can tell you that.'

'Ha.'

'How do you think a man on my pay keeps three kids at a private school, takes the wife to Dublin, and the kids to the seaside? New car?'

He leant eagerly towards the Major, his eyes fixed on the seamed face. The Major shook his head.

'I use my wits.' Mr Macken tapped the top of his head with a fat finger. 'Wits. Mind you, this is between ourselves.'

'Certainly.'

'In this job you'd be surprised what comes your way, if you're a man with his wits about him.'

'I've no doubts.'

The station-master leaned back in his chair and patted lovingly his breast-pocket; he'd more money in there than the old fella had in the bank. Buy him and sell him he could, if he felt so inclined. Wasn't all cake being gentry these days.

'That's a great bit of coal there.' He nodded at the leaping flames. 'Nothing like a good scuttle of coal. You never get warmth like that from th'ould turf.'

'No.'

'What's the situation like up your way?'

'Situation?'

'Fuel.'

'Oh . . . ah . . . yes. The usual wet turf.'

'They sell it too soon. Out for a quick profit.'

'We use our own wood mostly. Kelly always seems to be cutting down trees.'

'I could maybe manage to put a couple of tons of coal in your way. If you'd be interested, that is.'

'Well . . .'

'At, of course, no profit to myself. Nothing like coal for a good blaze.'

The Major sighed.

'Not just at the moment thanks, Macken. One way or another we're a bit . . .'

'Credit terms available.'

'. . . pushed. What with one thing and another.'

They supped their tea in silence for a moment. The Major's chilblains began to act up. He twitched his fingers peevishly.

'It's not often these days you come this way.'

'I've a little call.'

'Your mother, God rest her, was a great one for travelling. I mind well the time, and I a young porter, she would be coming and going all the time. A great restless woman. Rugs, boxes, and bags all over the platform.'

And, he thought to himself, she was a most unsatisfactory tipper.

'Times have changed,' said the Major.

'Minnie'd be a big girl now.'

'Sixteen.'

'Bless her.'

'Just finished school.'

'What'll she be doing then?'

The Major shrugged.

'God knows. She's just been spending Christmas with the General in London. I had hoped she'd get it into her head to stay over there.' He rubbed at his feverish fingers.

'My two eldest are over there now.'

'Ha.'

'And the girl mad to go, only her mother won't let her. Good money they're making.'

'I'm sure.'

'Never see them from one year's end to the other.'

'That's the way with the young. Spread their . . . ah . . .'

'Never fancied to go there myself, somehow.'

'. . . wings.'

They sipped and stared into the flames, their faces shining with the heat. Best English coal, nothing like it, beckoning with golden fingers.

'You can't stop them nowadays. If they want to do something they do it. And to hell with their parents. I could have fixed them up here with something if they'd stayed. But they wouldn't hear of it. It's their mother misses them. Worries. It's a terrible place for trouble over there.'

The Major cleared his throat. These days phlegm settled with too much ease around his vocal cords. He had to use his handkerchief. The bloody weather got you down.

'When are they closing you here?'

'Next year. So they say. I'll believe it when it happens.'

'What'll you do?'

'I have outside interests. And I'll have the pension. Jimmy in the box will maybe have trouble, though. They said they'd try and place him on the buses, but you never know.'

'It's a disgrace. If they pulled their socks up in Dublin and ran things more efficiently, they wouldn't have to close down country lines like this. Hardships.'

'True enough.'

'Never give a thought to anything outside Dublin. Develop Dublin and the industrial front and the rest can go hang.'

'True for you.'

'It's a scandal.'

'It's politics you should be in, Major.'

Somewhere a bell clanged. The station-master stood up and reached down his hat from a hook on the wall. He put it carefully on his head.

'That's the bell from the Halt. She'll only be a couple of minutes now. Don't stir yourself. I'll tell Minnie you're here.'

'No. No. I'll come. Thanks all the same.'

He drained down the remains of his tea. A pile of fat black tea leaves covered the bottom of his cup. Paradise for the fortune-teller. There was a distant whistle. Mr Macken went out on to the platform, pulling the navy collar of his uniform coat up round his ears as he went.

'All the best, Major.'

The Major put his cap on the table and took his time about getting to his feet. Old bones ache if moved too quickly. He looked at himself for a moment in the glass that hung over the fireplace, 'Guinness is good for you' stamped in gold letters across the centre. He looked terrible. Circulation all to hell. Must pop up to Dublin soon and have a thorough check-up. He looked old. No medicine men could do anything about that. He pulled his check cap out of his pocket and put it on, pulling the peak well down over his tender eyes. He hawked and spat into the fire, which sizzled angrily back at him. He turned to the window. Jimmy's signal was at green. The lights were on now in the box, and he could see the grey figure leaning on the handle, like a barman pulling a long pint. The train came round the corner. The smoke bursting out of it was almost black, and filled with whirling galaxies of golden sparks. The Major went out on to the platform and looked up at the line of lighted windows. There weren't more than twenty people on board, and no sign of Minnie anywhere. A knot of anger formed in the back of his throat. Somebody'd boobed and, as usual, he was on the receiving end. Damned if he'd come back tomorrow. What did they all think, anyway? That he'd nothing better to do than meet trains all day long? He chewed savagely at the corner of his moustache.

'Uncle Proinnseas.'

He turned quickly, his face under the cap reddening. What did she think she was doing, shouting that ridiculous name all round the station like that? Down by the guard's van she stood, bunched like an untidy parcel into her grey school coat, a long navy scarf twisted round her head. She waved, and jumped suddenly, with either cold or excitement, as he turned. Slowly he raised a hand and went towards her.

'Ha. Minnie.'

He stopped and she threw her arms around his neck.

'Uncle Proinnseas.'

He pecked at her warm cheek and untwined her arms. Making a show of him.

'Don't call me that ridiculous name.'

'You honestly thought I wasn't on the train, didn't you? I saw you looking savage.'

'I couldn't see you.'

'I was with Paddy in the van. We had tea and ham sandwiches. What a night to come home. Noye's fludde.'

'It's been like this for weeks.'

'Oh well, let's look on the bright side, maybe it'll make my hair curl.'

Paddy swung two large cases out of the van on to the ground at their feet.

'Evening, Major.'

'Evening, Paddy.'

'Bad night.'

'Ha. Is that the lot, Minnie?'

He felt in his pocket for a suitable coin. Half a crown it would have to be, taking the tea and sandwiches into consideration.

'Beastly,' said Minnie, kicking one of the cases very hard with the toe of her shoe.

'We'll burn them ceremonially the moment we get home. The end of an era.'

The coin passed hands and Paddy winked at the Major.

'You'll have your hands full now she's home for good.'

'Yes,' said the Major. 'How's the wife?'

'Famous. I'll tell her you were asking.'

'Well, Minnie, if that's all, there's no use in standing round here in the cold. Can we manage without a porter?'

'Of course.'

'Don't hurt yourself.'

'Don't fuss.'

He bent and picked up the larger case of faded green. It had seen him, almost certainly her father, through school. Ivy had dug it out of the attic and scrubbed away the smell of mildew, and it had started once more on the familiar journeys, back and forth. 'F. E. MacMahon' was printed on it, in shining black letters. He unlocked the Ford and with a certain effort lifted the two cases on to the back seat. Minnie settled herself into the well-hollowed bucket seat in front and reached over into the back for the rug.

'No.'

The tone of her uncle's voice startled her. She withdrew her hand and stared at him. He coughed and fiddled with the edge of his moustache. His fingers looked swollen and sore.

'I'll get it for you.'

'I can manage. Don't worry.'

'I said I'll get it. Didn't you hear?'

Almost roughly he pushed her arm off the back of the seat and leant over into the back. After a moment he pulled the rug up from the floor and settled it round her.

'Will you be all right?'

His voice was apologetic.

'Of course. Thank you.'

He banged the door and walked slowly round the car and let himself into the driver's seat. He groped on the shelf for his brown leather gauntlet gloves and pulled them on. Minnie watched him silently.

Hucka-hucka-hucka . . .

He let go of the starter and waited a minute.

'Uncle Bertie has a super new Jag.'

Hucka-hucka-hucka . . .

'Hmm.'

'He says he can do over a hundred in it. No problem.'

Hucka-huckahucka-hucka . . .

'I got his goat a bit by saying that I was sure they fiddled the speedometers to make you think you were going faster than you really were.'

Hucka . . .

'Don't you think that's highly likely?'

'Damn.'

'I'll swing it for you.'

She put out her hand to open the door.

'You'll do nothing of the sort.'

'But . . .'

'For God's sake, child, don't argue.'

'Have it your own way.'

Hucka. He pulled the starter angrily and the engine caught. Everything vibrated for a moment, then the Major rammed the gear in and they were off.

A long silence on the dark, twisting roads. From time to time the Major cleared his throat. He drove so close to the left-hand ditch that the lower branches of the trees tapped sometimes, like skeleton fingers, on the window by Minnie's face. What a night to come home. The swinging wind was out to meet her. Giving her a civic reception. She smiled slightly, graciously raised her hand in acknowledgement. She unwound the school scarf and shook her head to loosen her black hair.

'Something must be done about that mess.' Aunt Katharine's Knightsbridge voice spoke in her memory. 'I'll make an appointment for you with my girl in Harrods.' Mute appeal to Uncle Bertie, easy to handle, fond of spoiling little girls. He spoke round his cigar.

'Leave it, Katharine. It's charming. She's a real colleen. Buy her a red petticoat, but don't touch her hair.'

Grateful eyes in his direction.

Then home. Sighing for her. Unseen hands pulling constantly at the hem of her dress.

'We hoped that you would look upon this as your home too.'

'You're kind. But I want to go home.'

'What will you do there? There's nothing to do. Nobody.'

'I'll find something.'

'And, of course, Frank . . .'

'What about Uncle Frank?'

'He's not the most suitable person to bring up a girl of your age.'

'He's managed pretty well so far.'

'It's different now. You're not a child any longer.'

'Then I can look after myself.'

Exasperated sigh.

'I know a perfectly delightful secretarial college. What are you laughing at?'

'The idea that any secretarial college could possibly be delightful.'

Pursed lips.

'Bertie. You're the only one she listens to.'

'Leave the child alone.'

'It's ridiculous. She's far too young to make decisions that will affect her whole future life.'

'You can't make me stay here if I don't want to.'

'Quite. Don't go on at her, Katharine. Let her go home. After she's been there a couple of months she'll be sick of the place. If she's any sense.'

'You Irish have no sense of responsibility. If she was my child . . .'

'You wouldn't be having this tiresome argument. Like all the others she'd go straight into your blasted secretarial college without a murmur.'

'If you didn't approve of what the girls did when they left school, why didn't you speak?'

'Because they didn't need me or my advice. They were well brain-washed into being nice, well brought up bores. This, thank God, is Pat's child.'

'A great recommendation.'

'Katharine!'

His well-fed fingers crumpled into her hair. His interested lips brushed her cheek. She smiled up at him.

'I can go?'

'Of course, my dear Minnie. But make sure you come back and visit your old uncle before he gets too old to enjoy your company.'

The unremarkable burn that had curled its way along the valley beside them passed under a bridge and suddenly was transformed into the lough, heaving and swirling out into the mist. The road ran by the loughside a while, and the sharp smell of seaweed reached Minnie's nose. Just in sight, four white shapes tossed on the waves.

'Look, Uncle Frank,' she broke the silence, 'the children of Lir.'

'Ha,' said the Major.

Her words seemed to have released something in him. His hand groped out and patted her knee.

'It'll be good to have you home again.'

'Thank you.'

'Ivy's looking forward to seeing you.'

'How is she?'

'The same. Don't know what we'd do without her.'

'Darling Ivy.'

'Ha.'

He wrenched the wheel, and they spun round a corner, missing the whitewashed wall of the Gortnaree National School by inches.

'Nearly home,' gasped the Major, alarmed by his own recklessness. 'I hope we make it.'

Minnie put out her hand and touched the St Christopher medal fastened to the middle of the dashboard. The village houses leaned against each other, a row of old friends, staring across the narrow road at the waves. The windows glowed, and bright lights patterned the road from the open shop doors. A small pier curved out into the water, and a few boats bobbed below the grey stone wall. Up behind the village the mountain rose into the clouds, and on the gentle, cultivated slopes at its foot stood the two churches. Just off the road leading on to the Major's house, the Protestant church crouched like a little old lady, embarrassed at being found some place she had no right to be, behind a row of black yew trees. The other end of the village, on a slight eminence, a semi-cathedral topped by an ornate gold cross preened itself triumphantly.

'I take it brother Bertie was well?'

'Fabulous.'

'Katharine?'

'Bossy as ever.'

'Ha.'

'They sent their love.'

'Ha.'

'They seemed to expect me to stay. This wasn't some beastly plot of yours, was it?'

'The subject had been . . . ah . . . raised.'

'Uncle Frank.'

They had turned away from the lough, and the high stone wall of the Major's estate ran along the right-hand side of the road. Great gaps in it had been stuffed with brushwood, and piles of stones, where the wall had caved in, lay in the ditch.

'Your aunt has views.'

'I've heard most of them.'

'She has been pestering me by post. Hardly dare to open a letter with an English stamp.'

'What are your views?'

'Well . . . ah. Well . . .'

Minnie waited. He seemed to have finished. The wall was really in a terrible state.

'Well?'

'Whatever you like, really.'

'I want to know what you think. If you don't want me, I'll go straight back. Now. Tonight.'

'Who said anything about my not wanting you?'

'You're being so dreadfully incoherent.'

'This is your home. Of course we want you here. But your aunt is worried, and, indeed, I am too, about what is the best thing for you. In England there are . . . ah . . . opportunities.'

'All Aunt Katharine wants to do is cut my hair, polish me up a bit and get me married to some loathsome, eligible Englishman.'

'I think you're being a little . . .'

'I'm not. It's what she's done with her own daughters. Uncle Bertie agrees with me.'

'. . . unfair. I think she means well.'

'She's so awful.'

'Yes.'

'Uncle Bertie's an old pet.'

'Yes.'

'But she's really truly awful.'

'That's fixed then?'

'Yes.'

He swung the car rapidly across the road and through the gates.

'Home.'

'Oh yes, home.'

The elm branches creaked above them, like unoiled hinges, in the wind. Up round the house, the highest branches of the trees held uncountable numbers of rooks' nests, great black balls thrown up and caught by boney fingers; not even the strongest gale could prise them loose. Morning and evening, the rooks would rise up in a black cloud and hover over the trees screeching and screaming, and then, at some mysterious signal, they would sink lazily down and return to their nests.

The Major turned the engine off and put his hand on the horn, which coughed apologetically and made no other sound.

'Battery.'

The door was flung open and golden light flooded the steps and the gravel sweep. The block of Ivy's figure filled the doorway.

'Is it yourselves at last. I had yez in the ditch.'

Arms outstretched.

Minnie was out of the car in a flash and up the steps, buried in warm flesh.

'Ivy.'

'My baby.'

'It's so great to be home.'

'Dotey.'

The Major watched a moment, nibbling at his moustache. Displays of female warmth he found faintly displeasing. His throat was dry, demanding. 'I think,' his voice crackled up the steps towards them like radio static, 'the sensible thing to do is to adjourn . . . ah . . .'

Minnie felt a bumping against her leg and looked down to meet the hot brown eyes of the Major's labrador bitch smiling up at her.

Foetid breath rose from between her rotten teeth.

'. . . indoors.'

'Hello, you smelly old beast. Imagine you being still alive.'

She patted the black head, and the animal's back legs performed an ecstatic dance.

'Cold,' screeched the Major, banging the car door.

'Clever, clever girl. She knows me, Ivy.'

'And why shouldn't she?'

'Softening of the brain.'

'Get on with you.'

'Stinky, stinky.'

'The house is rapidly losing all its heat.' The Major pushed past them into the hall. 'Leave the cases,' he threw over his shoulder, 'I'll see to them in a few minutes. Must just . . .'

He disappeared down the hall, and Ivy sighed and pulled Minnie into the house, as she heard the boot-room door creak open and shut. The wind got under the red strip of carpet, now featherweight with age, that lay across the flagstones, and it fluttered like a flag in a sharp breeze. Ivy slammed the hall door behind her. The house smelt of turf smoke and distant meat cooking.

'There's a fire in the drawing-room. You must be famished.'

The fire glowed through a yellow mist of smoke. Eyes watered slightly. The turf sods were arranged with precision on the flat hearth. The flames climbed up inside the structure towards the dark chimney. Ivy stooped and threw a log on top of the smouldering turf. The smoke swirled angrily and then, with a wild crackle and an explosion of sparks, the wood caught.

'Did you have a good journey?'

'Grim. I got sick on the boat.'

'Ah sure, God help you.'

A spark jumped from the fire on to the hearth rug. Ivy killed it with her foot. The rug was freckled with small burns.

'The sea was like this.'

Minnie waved her arms round extravagantly, then unbuttoned her coat and dropped it on the floor.

'I thought my last hour had come. The dreadful thing about being seasick is that you really want to die. Pray for it. Hideous night of all time.' She crossed the room and threw herself into a chair beside the fire, feet on the fender stretched out towards the blaze. 'I'm dead.'

'You'll burn your shoes.'

'Who cares!'

'Ttt.'

Minnie toed her shoes off and returned her stockinged feet to the fender. 'It's smashing to be home.'

'Whatever they taught you over there, it wasn't tidiness.'

Ivy stooped and groped for the shoes. As she moved, her heavy body creaked, as if she was made of stuffed leather. She picked up the grey coat and shook it, then hung it over her arm. Minnie scowled at it.

'That can go, anyway. Big, big bonfire.'

'Nothing of the kind, my girl. Mrs Kelly'll be glad of it.'

'No one on earth would be glad of that beastly rag.'

'Beggars can't be choosers. There's warmth in it yet. You'll get chilblains if you put your feet in the fire like that.'

'After eight years of school in England I am immune to chilblains.'

'Look at your uncle.'

'He's old.'

'Only relatively speaking. What did they teach you over there, anyway, in eight years that you couldn't have learnt over here?'

'Things.'

'That's what you'd have learnt here, too, and not half the money draining out.'

Minnie closed her eyes and began to chant softly:

'I wandered lonely as a cloud
That floats on high o'er vales and hills,
When all at once I saw a crowd,
A host of golden daffodils,
Beside the lake, beneath the trees,
Fluttering and dancing in the breeze . . .

'I can go on.'

'Save your breath.'

'I don't remember much else.'

'You've filled out.'

'It's the age for filling out.'

'Did you have a nice Christmas?'

'Beastly.'

'There's gratitude for you,' said Ivy, with a certain triumph. 'Still and all, I told him you wouldn't like it.'

'Aunt Katharine bought me a whole heap of new clothes.'

'And if I know anything about it, you'll never wear any of them. They'll moulder in the press above. I had the week off. Went to my niece in Athenry.'

Minnie sat up. 'But Uncle Frank?'

'What about him? I don't know how she lives down there at all, it's a terrible place.'

'What happened about him?'

'You remember Sheila?'

'Do shut up about your niece. Ivy. How could you possibly leave him all by himself?'

'No nasturtiums cast in my direction, please. He just came one day and ordered me out of the house, and I having spent every Christmas here for twenty years. I'll not be needing you over

Christmas, says he to me. Just those very words. Where would I go, Major? says I to him. Just answer me that one if you can. Away off, says he, to your Sheila in Athenry, you're always complaining you never see her. Maybe she won't have me, says I. We'll cross that bridge when we come to it, says he. Adamant he was. So I went. I couldn't get him out of my mind all week. I'd had enough of Sheila and those screaming kids after a day, but I stayed the week out to give her a break.'

'But what did he do?'

'Your guess is as good as mine. The state of the house when I got back was enough to turn your stomach.'

'It's all very odd.'

'Ordered out, I was. So don't you go laying it all at my door. I'd better get on with the dinner. You'll be needing to go to bed early.'

'Mmmm.'

Ivy creaked out of the room, carrying Minnie's clothes. The bitch put her chin on Minnie's knee and panted happily. The wind rattled the long windows, and the brown velvet curtain stirred gently. The black tail thumped rhythmically on the floor. Somewhere a door shut. The wood on the fire cracked, spat a shower of sparks up the chimney. The door opened and the Major came in. He had taken off his greatcoat. His feet shuffled across the floor in brown felt slippers. His soft grey hair flopped exhausted on his forehead.

'Well,' he asked. 'All well?' He looked nervously across the room at Minnie as if he expected her to ask him to leave at any minute.

'Nothing's changed.'

His fingers pushed the soft hair away from his eyes. Even out of the cold they still watered, and the patch of skin below his eyes, where nose and cheek joined, shone damply. He looked as if he needed glasses. Minnie remembered how frightening his glittering eyes used to be when he was angry. Now it was as if she was looking at the blue of them through layers of gauze . . . He had changed, or perhaps she had changed in the last six months, not just her body, but her seeing eye. He must be well over sixty. He wasn't wearing well, though. Uncle Bertie, only two years younger, was well preserved. A fine figure, upright, clipped, groomed, his 'beautiful Irish skin', as Aunt Katharine called it, pink and finely lined. They both had the same hair, though, straight and soft, like a very small boy's, only stone grey. She smiled.

'Uncle Bertie goes to a royal hairdresser. By appointment, over the door.'

'What's that?' He fumbled for the arm of his chair. The bitch's tail thumped faster.

'I think it's rather funny.'

He lowered himself into his chair. 'What's that? Funny?'

'He gets green stuff in a bottle, that he . . .' She made the gesture of massaging her scalp. Her uncle stared at her with surprise.

'Ah, yes.'

'I brought you a bottle as a present.'

'Never use the stuff.' He pulled himself together. 'Kind of you. Thoughtful.'

'Eucris, it's called.'

'Splendid stuff. Wanted some for ages.' He began to peel off his mittens. His fingers were driving him mad.

'I called it "Eucharist" once, as a joke, and Aunt Katharine nearly bit my head off.'

'Ha. Yes. She would.' He pulled at his knuckles. 'Don't let that infernal dog annoy you.'

'She's not. You've let her get disgustingly fat. She'll drop dead of heart disease one of these days if you're not careful. And the stink is repulsive.'

'She's past her prime. Well.' He considered, calculated. 'I got her the year Pat . . . yes.' He looked quickly away from her towards the fire. 'She must be rising thirteen. Yes. Hardly in the first flush. Ha.'

'Poor old Tess. You and I arrived into the house together. I've worn better than you. At least I don't stink.'

'I've asked Kelly to look out for another one for me. Can't be without a dog. Might find one when I pop down to Dublin.'

'When are you thinking of going?'

He looked vague. 'Visit long overdue. Might go down to the Show. Have a look around. See a few old . . .'

'It would be a nice change for you.'

'. . . friends.'

'How are the Kellys?'

'No change. Mrs Kelly expecting.'

'Oh no.'

'I have two of the boys working for me now. If you can call it working.'

'I knew Kevin was.'

'Cormac has joined us. A mixed . . .'

'Cormac?'

'Yes. As far as I can make out he gets three pounds ten a week for whistling through his teeth, and spends what his father doesn't snatch from him on gaspers. Stunt his growth.'

'But he's only a kid.'

'Fourteen. Left school just before Christmas. Kelly prevailed upon me to take him on.'

He sighed, fingers scratching busily. The warmth from the fire had got his blood moving again. Warmth inside and out. Bloody back was cold, though. Draughts.

'I'm a . . . what d'ye call it, a sucker. I couldn't say no. Can't really find the money for any of them. It's not as if any of them did any work, either.'

'Kevin's a nice boy.'

'His heart's in the highlands. His heart is not here,' muttered the Major, somewhat enigmatically.

'Your dinner's on the table.' Ivy poked her head round the door.

'Ha.' The Major rose to his feet with surprising agility and headed for the door. 'Two minutes, I beg. Only two. Seat . . .'

He disappeared into the hall. Ivy frowned after him.

' . . . yourself.'

The boot-room door banged.

Minnie followed Ivy across the hall. Three tigers leered from the red damask walls, and tasselled swords hung criss-cross. At the foot of the stairs stood a small suit of armour, which looked as if it must have belonged to a child not more than ten. Minnie always avoided looking at it, as she was convinced that if you opened the visor and peered in, the owner would sourly peer back at you, enraged at having been canned for four hundred years. A salver squatted on the hall table, claw feet neatly turned out, waiting hopefully for the visiting cards that never came these days. Under the table a large bowl with 'DOG' written on it held water for Tess.

The dining-room was a fraction warmer than the hall. A small electric two-bar fire was placed equidistant between the Major's chair and Minnie's. It blistered the legs of the Nelson chairs, but did very little else.

Minnie sat down and unfolded her starched napkin.

'You never told me that Mrs Kelly was expecting again.'

'It's a disgrace.'

At the sideboard, Ivy heaped Minnie's plate with mutton chops and sprouts and great big floury potatoes bursting from their skins, and put it down in front of her.

'I couldn't possibly eat all that.'

'Don't wait for the Major. It'll only cool on you.'

Minnie picked up her knife and fork.

'It's a disgrace, and the baby only eight months. I told the Major he should speak to Kelly about it. But, of course, not a word.'

'It's hardly Uncle Frank's business.'

'That poor woman. Apart from anything else, she never knows where the next bite of food is going to come from.'

'I mean to say, Uncle Frank can hardly go to him and tell him to stop sleeping with his wife.'

Ivy looked outraged. 'Such talk.'

'Well, what else did you want him to do?'

'If that's the way young girls talk over there, your uncle would have done better to have kept you at home. Go easy with the butter.'

'Potatoes are unbearable unless they're swimming in butter.'

'Well it costs six shillings a pound over here, so not so much of the swimming, if you please. I'll tell you one thing, though.'

'Mmm.'

'There's two girls in the last year had to go over there because of him.'

Minnie didn't get it. 'To England?'

Ivy nodded. 'Two. No less. And you mind what I say, there'll be another before long, from what I hear around. He's a ram. That's what he is.'

'I must say, you're a nice one to be ticking me off for dirty talk. This is delicious.'

'There's things you can say and things you can't say. One thing about me, no one's ever complained about my cooking.'

The Major crept into the room and sat down. He tucked his napkin under his chin, like a Frenchman. Ivy put some food on to his plate.

'I'll say no more,' she said, broad back to the room.

'What's this?'

'Ivy was just saying that Mr Kelly's a ram.'

The Major flexed his itching fingers distractedly, and cleared the phlegm from the back of his throat. Ivy plonked his plate down in front of him.

'I've a right to voice my thoughts.'

The Major's voice was slightly blurred when it came. 'I . . . ah . . . think, in view of Minnie's . . . youth . . .'

Ivy ignored this. 'I've said it before and I'll say it again, it's up to you, and Father Murphy. It's no concern of mine that girls are getting impregnated in their hundreds and running over there. And that poor woman. No concern of mine at all. But it's up to you.'

'I really can't see why.'

'Aren't you his employer, and a man of education? And isn't Father Murphy his spiritual adviser?'

'I can't argue.'

'I wouldn't. I'll tell you one thing, though: if I was Father Murphy the first thing I'd do would be to cut him off from the body of the Church.'

Minnie giggled. Ivy glared at her coldly.

'Perhaps it wouldn't worry him,' suggested the Major.

'I'll say no more.' Ivy moved, deeply offended, towards the door. 'Not a word.' She left them to silence, and the staring ancestors in curling gilded frames.

The Major packed his fork full of food and pushed it into his mouth. You had to eat to keep going at all, but food disgusted him. He often wondered why one had this feeling, anyway, that you had to keep going. Hang on. Why? Because you didn't know. Had to push away the inevitable moment when you discovered all or nothing. Couldn't be worse than this lot, that was for sure. His hand trembled violently and the food fell off his fork back on to the plate again.

He looked up and saw that Minnie was watching him.

'What was that you said?'

She shook her head. 'I didn't say anything.'

'Oh. I thought . . .'

He put his knife and fork down side by side on his plate. Couldn't touch another bite.

'We'll have to see what we can do about it,' he said to her.

She didn't quite know what he meant, but she felt he meant well. She got up.

'If you don't mind. I'm whacked.'

'Not at all. Run along, by all means. You've had a long . . .'

She waited, but he never finished. She bent down to kiss him. Sharply he turned his face away, so that the kiss landed high up on his cheekbone. He patted her arm. She left the room and closed the door quietly.

He didn't move.

A Slight Explanation

About a hundred and fifty years earlier, a MacMahon had tipped his hat to the King of England, turned his back on Rome, and his fellow countrymen, and had been granted gracious permission to build himself a mansion house, in the grand style, on what had been, for many hundreds of years, his own land. His wife, an English lady of means and force, had imported an architect, garden planners, craftsmen, and on a gentle slope above the lough they had built a house in the English Italianate style. Cottages were pulled down to make place for the gardens. Ponds, flower-beds and pathways were built where once the peasants had grown potatoes. More cottages had to go, so that the views from the windows were not marred by the sight of poverty and squalor. The homeless people were rented (at what were, to the landlord, minimal rents) patches of mountainy land, on which to build their huts and scrape a living for themselves and their enormous families. 'The Irish breed like rabbits,' Mrs MacMahon had said once to some London friends, 'I'm told, indeed, when there's no food in the house they boil the baby.'

Mrs MacMahon, having finished her house, enjoyed the delights of wild country life for six months, and then decided she would die of boredom if she remained there another moment. So she, and her children and husband, removed themselves with all possible speed, to London, where life was more elegant and infinitely more amusing. A steward farmed the land for them, whose sole responsibility it was to see that they were well supplied with enough money each year to keep them in the style to which they were accustomed. No questions were ever asked as long as the money arrived at the appointed times. Altogether he was a most satisfactory employee.

From time to time the family visited the house, and the children ran wild in the park, the parents and their friends ate hugely and drank, and rode their thoroughbreds round the countryside, fished and shot and entertained the more civilized of their neighbours. In the park, the trees grew with dignity; beneath them the glossy horses cropped the grass, and for miles around the fields bordering the lough were filled in the summer with swaying golden corn. Golden corn, that filled the autumn grain ships, that left the pier at Gortnaree for English ports, that filled hundreds of hungry English bellies, that filled the pockets of Mr MacMahon, his sons, and their hardworking conscientious stewards.

The years passed. Nature, on the side of England's statesmen, solved their problems, caused by Irish overpopulation. Mr MacMahon and his wife died, leaving an eldest son of charm and gaiety, a handsome officer in a cavalry regiment. He was delighted at the opportunity of removing his wife and child from the scene of his most gallant battles, and sent them to live in Ireland, where he visited them for the hunting season, when his military duties permitted. It was on one of these visits that he designed the gates. Ornate, flamboyant, garlanded with carved flowers, they hung eight feet high between two stone pillars, topped by smiling lions. His design was executed by the estate carpenter — a shadow of a man, one of the few left in the mountain cottages after the famine. A silent man, who worked hard and took his pay, and never spoke; and then, one day his cottage was empty on the mountain. Another one had gone. Another roof sprouted grass and weeds, old wheels rusted in the yard. No one cared.

Nowadays the gates hung open, pale with weather and age. The avenue, that curved for half a mile under the tunnel of elms, was rutted and overgrown. The tiny, pillared gate lodge had not been lived in since 1922, when it had been the scene of one of the Civil War's minor incidents. Nettles grew up now through the empty windows, and in the height of summer foxgloves peered over the walls. No one any longer bobbed and smiled, or passed the time of day as the Major drove in and out.

Chapter Two

February 23.

For three weeks I have been so tired. Something to do with my age, I suppose. Even looking out of the windows seems to exhaust me. There's not much to see, anyway. The lough is grey on one side of us, the mountain grey on the other. The swans float past twice daily, with the tide. Somebody told me once that seagulls were dead sailors reincarnated. I wish they didn't mew like starving cats. In the fields cows swish their filthy tails. Uncle Proinnseas only appears for meals. He is much gloomier than he used to be. I do hope he hasn't got some terrible disease. I sometimes want to ask him, but never quite dare.

On my second day home I found, in one of the many unused bedrooms, a trunk full of my father's books. It had obviously not been opened since its arrival here and many of the pages have become spotted with damp. However, after several days drying out in front of the electric fire in my room, they are all legible. Luckily I was undisturbed by Ivy during the drying-out process, as the smell of mildew in my room was really very unpleasant. I do hope by the time I have got through the lot, approximately a hundred, that I will have filled many of the gaps in my education. The following authors are represented: Dostoievsky, Tolstoy, Tchekov, Turgenev, Gorki, Camus, Kafka, Orwell, Sartre, Gide, Marx (Karl),

Joyce, Lawrence, Yeats, Blake, Synge, O'Connor, Swift, Shakespeare, O'Casey. I intend to get Kevin Kelly to build me some shelves; until then, I have stacked them reasonably neatly on the floor. Each book has his name written in it, in small looping black writing not a bit like mine. I wondered whether to write my name below his, but decided against it. Altogether, it is a legacy I greatly appreciate.

I have been thinking hard about my future, but find it difficult to come to any conclusions. I hear Ivy scrubbing the hall; soon she will be up to knock on my door. That will be eight o'clock. Breakfast. Every morning it is the same. As Uncle Proinnseas says: 'I don't know what we'd do without Ivy here.'

*　*　*

Breakfast finished. The Major ate toast and marmalade in silence. Breaking his toast into small pieces, he spread the butter and the marmalade on each piece just the moment before he popped it into his mouth. Then, reaching for his cup, he washed each bite down with gulps of scalding tea. He opened his letters neatly, with an ivory paper knife laid each morning by his plate, pulled the letters half out of their envelopes, sighed at them and put them to one side. The *Irish Times*, though not the paper it used to be, was preferable. He propped it up against the hot water jug and immersed himself in its pages until his tea was finished, when he gathered everything up with his shaking fingers and shuffled across the hall to his study.

Minnie, in her red Jaeger dressing-gown, had her foot on the bottom step of the stairs.

'Where, may I ask, might you be going?' Ivy, a tray piled high with breakfast dishes, paused in her passage across the hall.

'Back to bed.'

'No,' said Ivy firmly.

'No?'

'No. We've had enough of this laying around like an out-of-work lady.'

Minnie looked injured.

'No need to put that look on your physiogamy.'

'What look?'

'You know as well as I do what look. Lounging, lazing. Let me tell you, in case you're not aware, them days are long past. Even dukes work nowadays.'

Behind the study door the Major coughed, and the pages of the *Irish Times* rustled like dead leaves in a winter wood.

'I've been reading. Furthering my education.'

'Yes. Well, you can further your education a little less and give me a hand around the place.'

'Oh Ivy . . .'

'Not a word. Away on up and dress. I'll be up with the accoutrements in a few minutes — and you can begin by giving your room a good turn out. You haven't touched it since you came home. I'm sure it's like a pigsty.'

Ivy continued on down the passage, waiting for no arguments. Minnie went up the curving staircase, two at a time. Slippered feet stamping one two, one two, on the threadbare turkey carpet. Slammed door, reverberating through the house. That would annoy the old troll anyway. Throwing on jeans, two sweaters to keep out the raw chill. Supposing she liked her room the way it was? That was her affair. My room. Not a child any longer to be pushed around. Who did she think she was, anyway? She sat down angrily in front of the silver-speckled glass and pulled at the tangles in her hair.

'All right.' The silver-faced ghost in the glass spoke. The comb paused in mid-air. 'This is it, then. Where do we go from here?'

Minnie put the comb on the dressing-table and shook her head.

'That's no answer,' snarled the ghost.

'I know.'

'Over three weeks you've been home, and no decisions made.'

'I've been so tired.'

'Excuses. Forgotten everything you've learnt, too, I'll be bound.'

'I wandered lonely as a cloud, that floats on high o'er vales and hills, when all at once I saw a crowd of golden . . .'

'I told you,' said the ghost triumphantly.

'Only a momentary aberration. You make me nervous.'

'Nonsense. Do you at least remember your own name?'

'Of course.'

'Well?'

'What is this anyway? Who are you?'

'The ghost of Christmas past. The wicked witch of the north. Anyone you care to mention. Name please.'

'Minnie MacMahon.'

'Parents.'

'Patrick MacMahon, deceased. Mary MacMahon, also deceased.'

'How, deceased?'

'In an air accident.'

'Where? When?'

'I don't know. An accident. I was only four. How could I know?'

'You might have enquired in the course of all these years.'

'My father doesn't seem to be anyone's favourite topic of conversation.'

'Father's occupation?'

'Journalist.'

'Would that be accurate and truthful?'

'Oh, I think so.'

'Have you never heard the whispers? A trouble-maker, a left-wing agitator, a writer of anti-capitalist, anti-colonialist, anti-British slogans on walls? Killed, not before his time, hurrying to some far-flung corner of the British Empire to foment trouble. Biting the hand that had fed him and his for centuries. A traitor to his class.'

Minnie picked up the comb again and pulled at the tangles with it. She looked coldly at the sneering face.

'How can you repeat such rubbish?'

'Everyone's entitled to their own opinion. To continue: mother's occupation?'

'None. Well, before she married my father she worked in a shop.'

'A shop?'

'Yes.'

'Hardly a shop, I believe. A hole in the wall in Baggot Street, Dublin, where she sold cabbages and bunches of ripe bananas to gentlemen in bedsitting-rooms.'

'I don't know what kind of a shop.'

'And your father, having well reached the age of discretion, married her. A tired left-wing agitator, rising forty. Taken by her pretty face. Her sweet smile, not unlike your own, beaten into her by the nuns.'

'You seem to know all the answers.'

'Incurring wrath.'

Minnie sighed.

'On both sides of the family.'

And sighed again.

'The last straw. Throw the cad out. The old lady didn't last long after.'

'You're too clever by half.'

'Excommunication. Crying to the priest. Prayers for lost souls. A nice pair, they were.'

'I wish you'd go away.'

'Four years of uncertain happiness. And then . . .'

'Bang.'

'Where do we go from here? You've a long time ahead of you to fill in. If you ask me, London's the place for you . . . learn typing, see a bit of life.'

'Oh, go back to hell, or wherever you came from.'

'Got your goat then, did I?'

Minnie clenched her eyes tight, and a million tiny stars burned and whirled inside her head. There was silence.

'I must be mentally unhinged,' she said aloud, opening her eyes and staring into the glass. Her own eyes stared back, the colour of summer waves, now blue, now green. She had always been displeased with her eyes, would have preferred a deep and brooding brown.

'A pigsty I said, and a pigsty I meant. Would ya looka.'

Minnie jumped. Ivy stood just behind her, staring around with distaste.

'You gave me a fright.'

'It's your nerves. It's no wonder you're a bag of nerves lying around with your nose in all those dirty books, wherever you laid hands on them.'

'They were my father's.'

Ivy sniffed. 'A crude, blasphemous lot, I'm sure, that a girl of your years shouldn't be stuck into. Anyway, it's running around outside you should be. It's a great pity the rector never married.'

'Mr Coffey?'

Ivy nodded. 'You'd have had his children to knock around with.'

Minnie giggled. 'You are funny.'

'That's a terrible noise. An English noise.'

'It's a noise made by adolescent girls the whole world over. I try to stop myself from doing it, but it slips out from time to time.'

She put a red hair-band on to her hair and looked at herself with interest. 'Do you think there's any possibility of my turning out beautiful?'

'No. A pretty face is a snare and a delusion. You're the image of your granny.'

'Which one?'

'None of your lip.'

'I think I'll go down to the village. Can I get you anything?'

'You're going nowhere till this room is done.'

She moved slowly across the room, bent down and pulled out the plug of the electric fire. Three sparks crackled.

'That fire's been on night and day since you've been here. Wait till your uncle gets the bill from the ESB, then there'll be ructions.'

'It's been so cold.'

'Aren't there two good fires below?'

'Look, I'll whizz round it with the Hoover when I come back from the village.'

'You'll whizz round it with the Hoover before you put your head out of this house.'

'OK. OK. Have it your own way.'

'And no sauce from you, either.'

Ivy's lace-up shoes, shined so you could see your face in them, squeaked as she crossed the room. Altogether she sounded like a poor one-man band – wheeze, creak, squeak, with each step. She bulged out of her navy wrap-round at all possible places. She opened the door and looked back at Minnie, then smiled, a curving, new moon of a smile. Minnie pushed a clip into the side of her hair.

'I had a most extraordinary experience,' she said.

Ivy's smile vanished.

'I think I saw a sort of a ghost.'

'It's dreaming you were.'

'No. Just a few minutes ago. Here.'

'Hallucinations.'

'I've come to an important decision. I'm going to be a writer.'

Ivy gazed at the ceiling for a moment. 'I hope you won't turn out like your father. Nothing but sorrow and trouble in his footsteps.'

A sudden burst of rain splattered against the window. Outside, the black trees shuddered and tried to free their branches from the burden of nests.

'I don't suppose I will.'

'You'd do better to concentrate on the domestic arts. A man would rather have a wife who can cook him a good dinner than one who sits tapping at a typewriter all day.'

'Then I'll probably never get married. I'm not really very interested in sex, anyway.'

'Ttt.'

There was a long silence. The electric fire ticked as it cooled down.

'The accoutrements are on the landing. See you do it well, or you'll only find yourself doing it again tomorrow morning.'

She left the room, tossing the ball to Minnie over her shoulder: 'Willamina Shakespeare!' A diminuendo of chuckles joined the band. Faded down the stairs.

'Damn!' said Minnie.

About eleven, dust-daubed, breathing heavily, and tangled in accoutrements, she heard the car cough in the avenue below. She shoved up the lower half of the window and leant out. Kevin Kelly stood almost to attention by the open car door. Greatcoat and cap descended the steps, slightly heavily, but with military tread. The hand up in half-salute.

'Morning, Uncle Proinnseas. Beastly day.'

Slam.

At the sound of her voice Kevin looked up and nodded in her direction. The car was away, a ribbon of blue smoke levitating behind it, knee-high. Kevin winked.

'Where has he gone?' Minnie asked Ivy as they sat down together to lunch in the kitchen. A large pearl bulb hung between them, under a white china shade. The smell of scorched clothes and bread in the oven had been the same for ever. Ivy had trouble with her teeth. Like the china shade, they shone, freshly laundered every day, but they had never fitted properly. Mainly for show, but not for serious eating. She lived mainly on potatoes and gravy, and polished and repolished her plate with hunks of white shop bread, held daintily between thumb and first finger. Then ginger biscuits, softened up in hot, sweet, stewed tea. The metal pot was constantly on the simmer, no one could pass through the kitchen without a cup of the poison being thrust into their hand.

'Donegal Town.'

Brief. Fill the mouth with floury spud, steaming, straight from the pot, no need to chew.

'Whatever for?'

Ivy shook her head.

'I wish I'd known. I'd have gone for the drive.'

Ivy swallowed. 'If he'da wanted you he'da asked you.'

'I suppose so. Except sometimes I think he forgets I'm here. Occasionally a look of complete surprise passes over his face when he comes into a room and finds me there.'

'He has things on his mind.'

'Do you want me to give you a hand with the washing up?'

Ivy shook her head. 'If you're going to the village you'd better get on before the rain comes on again.'

Fwut-fwut-fwut. Her head felt dizzy from stooping. The air seemed to be going in, anyway. And staying in, more important. Better bring the pump with her, just in case. Needed a drop of oil; maybe Kevin tomorrow might.

'Here.' Ivy put a large cardboard box down on the ground beside her. 'Some things for Mrs Kelly. Drop them in on your way past.'

Minnie pushed the lid open with the pump and peered in. 'It looks like a thousand pairs of school knickers.'

'There's warmth in them still.'

'My school knickers.'

'She'll be glad of them.'

'No, no, no.'

'What do you mean — "no, no, no"?'

'I absolutely refuse to carry charitable boxes of my . . . cast-off knickers to people.'

'There's a whole heap of other things, too.'

They glared into each other's eyes.

'Get on with it, then,' said Ivy and creaked back into the house.

The rain was over for the time being, blown away up the lough to the open sea, by a chilly, frisky little wind. Cold silver drops splashed from the branches as Minnie negotiated the ruts and puddles down the drive. Around her the fields lay, gorged with liquid, unconscious drunk.

The Kelly's cottage sat in a left-hand curve of the road, backing up against the Major's crumbling wall. A few hens rocked their way across the road to scratch in the ditch. A skin-and-bone dog looked up from where he lay, as the bicycle came round the corner. The roof had once been thatch, was now red corrugated, faded to pink. Two small windows and a door were set into the thick stone walls. There was nothing about the place to set the tourists' cameras clicking. A child was yelling its head off. Minnie propped the bike against the wall and knocked on the door. The dog rose slowly and padded over to her. He sniffed at her leg and turned away, disappointed. Almost at once, he sat down and began to scratch behind his ear. Minnie knocked again, then stopped and began to untie the box from her carrier. The door opened a crack and a small grey face appeared.

'Hello,' said Minnie.

The door closed again rapidly. Inside, the yelling increased in volume and then suddenly stopped. Voices. Minnie pulled at the string. She wondered whether to knock again. She wound the string into a neat ball and put it in her pocket. The door opened again. Kevin smiled at her.

'Hello,' she said again.

He was a head taller than her. Could have done with a light shave.

'It's great to see you home again.'

'Is your mother there?'

He nodded, and called back over his shoulder.

'It's all right, Mam, it's only Minnie.'

He looked at the box on the bike. 'She thought maybe you were the welfare.'

'Well, I'm not.'

'No. Will you come in?'

'Ivy asked me to drop some things in. They might come in handy.'

His eyes lit on the box again. The patches of bristle on his cheeks and chin were ginger. The same grey face as before poked round the door again. 'Me mammy says you're to come in.' It withdrew.

'There,' said Kevin. 'You'd best come in.'

'Just for a minute.'

'I'll take the box.'

He moved out of the doorway. She ducked her head and went in. He followed her, the box bumping against her back. Stinging, smoky blackness. Potatoes boiled in their skins for a hundred and fifty years, in black metal pots over the smouldering turf on the hearth. Damp walls. Damp clothes. Sweat. The box bumped her gently into the middle of the room.

'Mam!' yelled Kevin. He dumped the box on the table. Mrs Kelly came in from the back room, a small child, tear-streaked, balanced on her right hip.

'I heard you were home. You've grown.'

'How are you, Mrs Kelly?'

'I could be worse. I could be dead. Say "hello" to Minnie, Baba.'

Baba threw an arm around her mother's neck and buried her face in her shoulder.

'She's shy.'

'Ivy asked me . . .'

'She's brought some stuff down for the kids.'

He opened the lid and peered in. Minnie blushed.

'It's not much. Just a few old things of mine. Ivy thought they might come in handy.'

'Ivy never forgets us. God will reward you.'

Her voice had a real tinker whine to it. She shifted the child to her other hip. The little girl who had opened the door to Minnie crept up close and pulled at her sleeve.

'Wouldya have a penny?'

Her small, filthy hand waited.

'I . . .' Minnie groped in her pocket.

Mrs Kelly was over the floor in one jump and slapped the child hard across the face. Minnie's eyes watered at the sound of the blow. The child screeched.

'Let me get you up to those tricks again and I'll tan the hide offya.'

Like a jungle bird, the screeching went on. Mrs Kelly balled her fist and raised it threateningly: 'Let you shut up or I'll give you something to cry for.'

'Here.'

Minnie shoved a sixpenny bit into the girl's fingers. 'Get yourself some sweets.'

The child stopped crying. Her eyes flickered backwards and forwards between her mother and Minnie. Mrs Kelly was all smiles.

'Well, isn't that kind of the young lady. What do you say? Where's your manners?'

The child rubbed her cheek where her mother's fingers had left a red mark. She looked at Minnie, but didn't speak.

'That's all right. She doesn't have to say anything.'

'Give the money here to me and I'll mind it for you.' She stopped and pulled the coin from the child's fingers. The child only stared at Minnie. Minnie didn't dare speak.

'She'll only lose it.'

'Hey. Look here at me.'

Kevin stood behind the table dressed in Minnie's old school coat, a pair of navy knickers dangling rakishly over one ear. The sleeves of the coat came halfway down his arms, his hands stuck out like a marionette's from the tight grey tubes. The little girl transferred her stare to him. Minnie really blushed.

'Just what I've been wanting for years.'

'Get them off ya.' Mrs Kelly snatched the knickers off his head and pushed them into the box. 'Have ya no manners at all? Minnie'll think ye were dragged up.'

'It's just a few old things. Ivy thought . . . There's warmth in them yet. It seemed a pity to throw them away.'

'Yiz are kindness itself. They'll be great for the girls. That coat'll fit Bernie to perfection.'

'I hope so.'

'No doubt at all.'

'I'd better be getting on so.'

'Would ya not stay and have a cuppa tea? The pot's on.'

'No, thanks all the same. I have to go to the village. I think I'll get on before the rain comes.'

'You're going to the village?'

He'd taken the coat off and folded it up neatly. It lay on the table beside the box.

'Yes.'

'I'll be with you. I have to pick up some paint at the hotel.'

'OK.'

Mr Kelly ducked his way into the room from the back. His face was sleep-blurred. The sleeves of his striped flannel shirt were rolled to the elbow. Thick black hairs covered his arms, and exploded out through the opening down the front of his shirt. More like a monkey than a ram, thought Minnie.

'Is it too much to ask for quiet?'

'See who's here,' said his wife quickly.

'Hunh.' He peered in Minnie's direction. 'Is it Minnie?'

'The same.'

For no apparent reason, the baby began to cry again.

'Ssh, now.' Her mother swayed back and forth on the balls of her feet. Mr Kelly came over to Minnie and took her hand.

'Aren't you the grown-up young lady now. It's great to see you. You've been hiding away since you came home. Can you not shut that bloody child up, or take it out of here?'

Silently Mrs Kelly left the room, followed by the small grey girl.

'You can't hear yourself think with that racket. Did she even offer you a cup of tea?'

'Yes, thanks. I've got to go, though. I'm on my way to the village. I just dropped in . . .' She made an inadequate gesture with her arms.

'Just so.'

He stared at her for a moment. 'You're as pretty as a picture getting.'

'Thank you.'

She couldn't think of anything to say and stared at her feet. His eyes burned her up and down.

'And I know what I'm talking about.'

In the back room Mrs Kelly wheeled the baby to stop its noise.

'Ask anyone around and they'll tell you. Kelly knows what he's talking about, on that subject. That's right, isn't it, son?'

'Come on, Minnie. If we're going to the village, let's go.'

'I'm all set. Goodbye, Mr Kelly.'

She turned quickly for the door. Behind her she heard Mr Kelly move.

'What's this?'

'You heard.'

'Is it an afternoon off you're taking when the Major's back is turned?'

'You're a nice one to be talking.'

She was out into the air. The dog slept again. The hens disappeared through the hedge into the field beyond.

'You'll not talk to me like that.'

'Minnie's waiting.' Kevin appeared at the door. 'Will we go?'

Minnie nodded and took hold of her bicycle. She pushed it towards the corner. She could hear his steps behind her.

'One of these days I'll kill you.'

The door crashed.

'Don't worry, I'll never turn my back on you for long enough.'

He didn't dare speak the words above a whisper. He put his hand on the saddle. Minnie stopped walking.

'Do you want to walk, or will I take you on the carrier?' he asked.

'The carrier every time. If you've the strength. I'm no fairy.'

He bent forward and felt the tyre with his thumb.

'That'll do. Hop on, so.'

She got on to the carrier, conscious of staring eyes behind the dark window.

'Can I come wit yez?'

A red-haired boy, Minnie's shoulder high, appeared from the ditch, a butt glowing viciously and fading between his lips. Kevin turned his back and mounted the bike.

'Don't be forever trailing after me.'

'It's Cormac. Is it?'

Kevin grunted.

'Hello, Cormac.'

The boy shifted his feet, but didn't speak.

'You've got so big, I'd never have known you.'

Kevin twirled the pedal impatiently with his toe.

'I hear you're working up with us now.'

'If you'd get up there and show some signs of activity instead of hanging round me like a shadow.'

Cormac unstuck the butt from his lip and threw it on the ground. He put a boot on it to kill the last remaining spark.

'Can I not come?'

'No. I said no. Wash your ears in the morning and you'll hear better in the future.'

The little boy groped helplessly in his pocket for another cigarette. Kevin turned and looked at him.

'If you've nothing better to do you can go up and finish stripping them walls in the stables for me. I want to start in on the painting tomorrow.'

Cormac didn't reply.

'Are you right, Minnie?'

'Yes.'

'Here we go then.'

He pushed off with his foot and they wobbled around the corner, the bike dipping and swooping like a ship in a storm.

'Goodbye, Cormac,' she called back over her shoulder.

'Goodbye.' His voice was resigned, half man, half child.

Kevin had his balance now and settled on the saddle; the wheels swished beneath them.

'He's very young.'

'He's gone fourteen.'

'That's very young to be working.'

Panting breath.

'A fat lot of work he does.'

The road was iron-grey, a sunless river, winding its way along the skirt of the mountain. The bog stretched out level with the road for a few hundred yards before it began to rise gently, brown wounds open, patches of water reflecting grey clouds, neat stacks like little houses scattered here and there, wet with blobs of sheep, constantly on the move, above the rocks and winter-dull heather. Kevin had his second wind and his breathing was back to normal. The wheels crackled through rainbow-coloured puddles, and brown mud splattered their legs.

'Are you done with school now?'

'Yes.'

Her arms held him tightly. His legs whirled in a mad extravagance of speed.

'I thought you'd have been back for Christmas.'

'No. Worse luck.'

'What were you up to?'

'They wanted me to stay a while in London. With Uncle Bertie. They thought it would do me all sorts of good. And between you and me, I think they hoped I'd stay.'

'And did it?'

'What?'

'Do you all sorts of good.'

'I couldn't say.'

Who was to say? The Tate . . . The Old Vic . . . Orchestra stalls at the Garden . . . Tea at Fortnum's, scented ladies eating cakes with tiny two-pronged forks. Dinner parties with nice people in Chelsea. Stockbrokers, bankers, eminent men. Young Guards officers with white teeth and well-oiled smiles. His father's this; her father's that . . . I wouldn't have too much to do with her, dear, her father's not quite . . . Harrods . . . Concerts in the Festival Hall. Nothing but the best: Menuhin, Rostropovitch. Kathcen – my girls are nothing if not cultured. Where do your people live in

Ahland? . . . Flats in suitable neighbourhoods . . . Committees and junior committees, raising a few hundred in the most agreeable way possible for those unable to help themselves . . . The National Gallery – and then Fortnum's again, for morning coffee. Who was to say?

'What's it like?'

'Horrible.'

Ungrateful child, after all we've done for you. The hub of the world. The linchpin of the British Empire. God Save the Queen.

'Hunh?'

'Yes. Horrible.'

'Ah, come off it, Minnie. They say it's great.'

'Well, they can have it, whoever they are.'

'I've honestly heard it's great.'

'The streets are not paved with gold, in case that's what you're thinking.'

'Maybe not. But there's gold around just the same.'

'You're never thinking of flitting?'

'There'd be a bit of life.'

'I always thought you had more sense. Look, I'll tell you one super thing – the buses are red. That's the only thing in its favour. Lovely giant red, absolutely Technicolor buses. They move with such – oh, I don't know – massive dignity through the streets. They take their own time. Great they are. Higher than your house. Hundreds of them.'

'Fifteen pounds a week, I could earn, laying bricks, and not kill myself to do that, either. Be my own master.'

'Hollow men everywhere.'

'Cinemas, dances, a bit of gas.'

'Grey dust in the street, choking you. People . . .' She laid her cheek against the back of his jacket.

'Freedom. Money in your pocket. No questions asked. Girls in their thousands, like you see in the magazines, smiling at you.'

' . . . like cattle on a Fair day. Thousands of panicky cows let out of a pen.'

'Fifteen smackers – and overtime.'

'What do you want fifteen pounds a week for?'

There was a moment's silence. 'What does anyone want it for?'

'I don't.'

'You're only a kid yet.'

'I am not.'

'You are so.'

A long silence. A single fat drop of rain fell on Minnie's face. Round a bend, and they saw the neat spire of the Protestant church rising from its grove of trees.

'I've never had a bath. Just a small thing like that. You wouldn't ever think twice about. Never lived in a house with a tap, let alone a bath. A couple of weeks ago I was up at the house fixing a tap for Ivy, and I couldn't get the temptation out of my head to fill the bath up with boiling water and lay in it like a gentleman for half an hour or so. Right up to the neck.'

'It's never more than luke up there, anyway.'

She could have choked herself. He didn't seem to hear, though. His coat smelt of turf smoke.

'It's the whining kids most of all. They never stop. On at you all the time, screaming or whining, always on at you till your nerves are shredded. Under your feet night and day. Nowhere to go to get away, only out into the weather. And the old fella as bad, worse, battering the daylights outa her whenever he feels inclined. Nowhere to go. That's the point. Cormac's feet in your mouth when you turn over in the bed.'

'Can't you get some place of your own?'

He rang the bell and they turned into Back Street, sloping down towards the harbour.

'That's just what I intend to do. Over there. The Englishman's fifteen pounds and overtime will see me further than the Major's five pounds ten will ever do.'

'You sound so cross.'

'Demented. It's not cross I get, it's tight in my head somehow. Like I said, demented. Do you understand?'

'I suppose I do. Not too much really. We look at things from different angles.'

Four boys were leaning over the sea wall, throwing stones at a dead dog on the wrinkled sand below. The white waves curled and uncurled a hundred yards out. Half a dozen seagulls circled and screamed above the corpse, and the boys threw the odd stone in their direction. Kevin rang the bell again and the boys turned and leaned on their elbows, watching. One of them casually tossed a stone after the bike, and it rattled on the ground just short of the back wheel.

'Where's your destination, madam?'

'The Post Office.'

'I'll pedal you up there and then we can come back to the Hotel and collect the paint. It was left off from the Letterkenny bus.'

'Why didn't you tell your father what you were coming down for?'

'I wouldn't please him.'

The winter sun came out for a moment, and all the windows flashed.

'Look at that now,' said Minnie, delighted.

'What?'

'The sun.'

A large grey cloud pushed its way in front of it.

'You shouldn't mention the sun. It's like a shy child, always running behind its mammy's skirts when noticed. If you want it to stay shining pay it no heed.'

He drew across the road and put his foot down outside the Post Office . . . Ofig an Phuist in yellow on green above the door.

'I won't be a minute.'

Minnie got off the bike and crossed the pavement.

Some flight of fancy, years before, had inspired Miss May in the Post Office to paint her step silver. Every morning, seven to the dot, the bells of the two churches clashing, a little out of time, it got its scrubbing, and twice a year a new coat out of the tin. Minnie hopped over it, as she had always done. To put your dirty shoe on it would have been like standing on some delicate part of Miss May's body. Kevin smiled sourly as he watched her antic. The seagulls yowled like hungry cats. She was only a kid yet. Anyway, people like her never knew what the world was really like. Red as a beet when he'd put those old knickers on his head. She'd have laughed if Mam hadn't been there, though. What did he want with fifteen pounds a week? Sweet Holy Jesus, what a question to ask! It wasn't all that long since he'd been hopping over that step himself. Kid stuff. She hopped out again, and threw a bundle of notebooks and some ball-point pens into the basket fastened to the handlebars.

'I thought you'd finished with school.'

He turned the bike around and they began to walk back the way they'd come.

'I'm going to be a writer.'

He looked at her with surprise. 'Seriously?'

'Absolutely.'

'How do you begin?'

She picked nervously at her cheek with a finger. 'I don't know. Just sit down and write, I suppose, anything that comes into your head.'

'Stories and the like?'

Minnie nodded.

'I got marvellous marks in school for English. My only decent subject, really. My last report said that I let my imagination get the better of me at times, but that I showed remarkable ingenuity in phrase-making. I don't really know what they meant by that, but Uncle Bertie laughed and said, "Good on you."'

'Good on you?'

'An Australian phrase he'd picked up somewhere. He was rather hooked on using it. It meant he was pleased.'

'Oh.'

'Aunt Katharine, on the other hand, tutted. I think she thought I was a lost cause before I was begun. Uncle Bertie was really the only one who ever took a lively interest in anything I did. Mind you, I sometimes felt it was a bit too lively. You know men of that age.'

Kevin blushed this time. 'I don't know what . . .'

'Of course you do. You couldn't blame him. Living with Aunt Katharine wouldn't be much fun. I kept out of range.' She twitched her bottom gaily to one side, showing how to avoid an old man's fingers.

He pushed the bike up the hill holding only the saddle; it took a certain concentration to keep the front wheel straight. She skipped beside him to keep up, her wind-tangled hair swinging from side to side.

'But writing,' he asked, 'what made you decide on that?'

'I just thought I'd give it a try. It's in my blood.'

She laughed suddenly and turned, walking backwards beside him, the better to see his face. She waved her hands under his nose. Blue veins criss-crossed below the pale skin.

'Look at that. It's ink. A hundred times handier than blue blood.'

She stopped. He almost walked into her. The bicycle wheels swivelled and he had to catch at the handlebars quickly to prevent the bike falling.

'Don't you think it's an absolutely marvellous idea?'

'Can you not stop hopping up and down like that and walk like a normal person?'

She turned and walked beside him neatly. Across the road, on the sea wall, someone had written in large white letters: A VOTE FOR BRENNAN IS A VOTE FOR THE DEVIL. Minnie wondered what poor Brennan had done to deserve such adverse publicity, and was relieved to see that round the corner some undaunted follower of Brennan had scrawled: BRENNAN NUMBER ONE.

The hotel, salmon-pink and two-storeyed, stood on the corner opposite the harbour. A portico with fluted columns gave dignity to the doorway. Thick, hand-crocheted curtains kept the rooms suitably dark. Big Jim Breslin, the proprietor, now shrivelled and almost weightless, stood, and moved slowly from room to room, supported by a blackthorn stick. Without it he was helpless. A bundle of clothes heaped in a chair. Most of the day he spent sitting by the window of the lounge, peering through the curtains and the mist of age that veiled his eyes, at the comings and goings in the street. Most of the night he spent, unable to sleep, propped on four pillows, staring out of his bedroom window, across Back Street, at the ever-open side door of the Famine Bar. The memory of his fine days lay on his mind, like autumn leaves on the fields. He re-lived, in his chair, the splendours of the Rebellion and the tragedies of the Civil War. He had worn a black band round his sleeve for Michael Collins, until his wife had threatened to be seen no more in the street with him unless he took it off. He had refused to wear the same band for her, when she passed on one winter night, merely asking his daughter-in-law to sew a small black diamond on his sleeve. He waited now, with gentle impatience, for the beckoning finger, the hand on the shoulder, the reunion with the Chief. His only son, Little Jim, was the fat and prosperous manager of an hotel outside Birmingham, and his wife and kids spent a month each summer with the old man. 'They're fine kids and a credit to you,' Big Jim would say to his daughter-in-law, as he listened to the children's Midland accents in the dark rooms, 'but they're not Irish.'

Kevin propped the bike against one of the pillars. He pushed open the creaking door and held it while Minnie went past him into the darkness. Somewhere, sometime, cabbage had been boiling, and the smell, mixed with paraffin oil, tinted the air. Big Jim's voice called from the bar, and his stick tapped on the shining-brown, parquet-patterned lino.

'Is that yourself, Kevin?'

'It is an' all.'

'And a girl with you?'

He appeared in the doorway, stick clamped in arthritic hand. He peered up at Minnie, trying to place her.

'It's me, Mr Breslin, Minnie MacMahon.'

'Well, amn't I the old fool.' He shuffled forward and gripped her arm. 'A grown girl you are now.'

He stared into her face, reading each curve, each feature, like the racing page.

'The spitting image of your daddy, God rest his soul, you're getting to be. Amn't I truly the old eejit. Anyone mention Minnie MacMahon to me, and I see in my mind's eye a wild young one, and here you are, a young lady, bursting on me like a rose in June. Isn't she a sight for sore eyes?'

Kevin winked at Minnie and grinned.

'I wouldn't dare argue with you, Big Jim. It'd be as much as my job was worth.'

Minnie felt the stab of his smile down near her stomach. She clenched her teeth angrily. That was something she needed like a hole in the head. No mooning and moping for her. No. Not for Minnie. No wallowing in uncontrollable emotion. No adolescent sighing. Keep a tight hand on yourself, girl. The humiliation. The waste of time spent suffering needlessly. Not a stab, not a shiver further must it go.

'Come on in. If it'll tempt you to stay a while, I'll stand you both a ginger.'

His plucking fingers on her sleeve drew her into the bar. Kevin followed reluctantly.

'Your dadda spent a lot of time in here, one way or another.'

Kevin gave a little spurt of knowing laughter. The old man turned and shook his head.

'Don't go getting me wrong, son.' He moved slowly behind the bar, each step a pain all through him. 'The spitting image, you are.'

Minnie perched herself on top of one of the three-legged cocktail stools, almost the only concession in the hotel to the tourist drive, and watched Big Jim reach down two stone bottles of ginger and pour the contents, steaming into two tumblers. He pushed them across the bar.

'Compliments of the house.'

'Thanks.'

'All kids are the same, they love that stuff.'

Kevin scowled and lifted the glass to his lips. He sneezed as a million bubbles rushed up his nose.

'No,' said Big Jim, 'don't go getting me wrong. He just felt it was home here.' There was a moment's silence. The old man sighed. 'Them old airioplanes are desperate things.'

'I don't remember him at all,' said Minnie.

'Ay. His home it was. Like a son, he was. Spoke more to me, indeed, than me own son ever did. In here all the time with his troubles, since he was a little fella. They weren't exactly great with each other up there. We could have done with more like him in the trouble times.'

With enormous care he drew himself a Guinness and placed it

on the bar. His hands trembled with each movement.

'I've all his published writings in the box below.'

'I'd love to have a look, sometime, if it isn't inconvenient.'

'It's likely you would. Time enough, though; there's things there would be above your understanding.'

He drank. Wiping the froth from his lips afterwards, with his twiglike fingers. Kevin stirred restlessly beside Minnie.

'If it's politics you mean, I can tell you that for my age I am very politically aware. I used to read the *New Statesman* at school. Clandestinely, you understand.'

'I can see him now.'

The old man stared fixedly at the door. Minnie turned furtively, though she knew she would see nothing.

'He'd stand in that door shouting my name, till I came running from whatever part of the place I might be in, and everyone else, too, to get a loog at the carry-on. "It's the prodigal son, the renegade, Red Paddy demanding a suitable welcome." Then, he'd pick me up, and there was more weight on me in those days, and kiss me on both cheeks, yelling between smacks to the girl for Jamesons all round. Never went near the house after the trouble about the girl. Your mother . . . Never went further than the gates. He'd go up some nights and have a look at them. Then he'd come back here, cross as two sticks, and as like as not, drink himself and all the rest of us under the table. Things were really lively when he was around, I must say that.'

His shrunken head barely cleared the bar top. The Guinness was distasteful. He pushed it away from him, as a child a glass of unwanted milk. Even his pleasure in drinking was gone. He couldn't even take enough now to get drunk and hurry the minutes on.

'Did you ever meet my mother?' asked Minnie tentatively.

He shook his head. 'He never brought her up here. I advised him agin the whole thing, right from the start; but he wouldn't heed me. It wasn't only his family would like to have seen him well married.'

Minnie twisted her glass on the bar, and said nothing. His grave-cold finger touched her cheek with apology.

'I'm sure she was a fine girl. But all the same, she wasn't his class, and hard and all as the old lady was, it broke her heart. She was never the same after. So the word has it.'

Over the door that led to the kitchen, the Virgin Mary, blue-robed, held out her arms to sinners. A red lamp burnt, with a sweet smell, at her feet.

'I knew beginning and end of that man. More than I'll ever know of my own son. It makes me feel very old.'

Minnie thought how they'd only need a child's coffin to put him in when he went. Indeed, if he grew much smaller he would just blow away one windy day, helter skelter down the street, like a torn scrap of newspaper. Outside, someone whistled 'Pedro the Fisherman'. Kevin kicked a boot against the bar impatiently.

'It's time we were getting on.'

'I'll never see eighty again. I've seen so many go.'

The bird's head shook sadly on the thin neck. His veiled eyes were better suited now for seeing the dead rather than the living.

'Ay,' he muttered, 'ye had better be getting on. You'll be wanting the paint.'

'No hurry,' said Minnie. 'The Kelly family are taking things easy today. Uncle Frank's gone to Donegal Town.'

Kevin kicked the bar again, and then saw the grin on her face. He grinned back at her. Her eyes moved away from him quickly.

'Is that where he's gone off to? I saw the car pass the window this morning. No one ever sees the Major these days.'

'He's becoming a bit of a recluse all right.'

'Ay.'

'I'd have a Harp if we weren't moving,' said Kevin.

The old man reached down a bottle of Harp and a glass. He took the lid off the bottle of Harp and passed it over to the boy.

'I hope you're not taking after your father.'

'I've more sense.'

'I'd hope.' He turned and blinked at Minnie again. 'Ay, it's Minnie, all right.'

She smiled. 'It's me.'

'He'd do just that.'

Minnie followed his eyes down to her fingers twisting round the glass.

'Couldn't keep still a minute. A bundle of nerves. He felt we'd all turn agin him when he joined the British Army, and he'd come up here on his leave and sit there trying to explain. "I'm not fighting for the British Empire, Big Jim," he'd say, twisting his fingers just like you're doing now. "I'm fighting against Fascism. The most evil thing that's ever happened to the world." Those were his very words. "I'm trying to consolidate the freedom we got for ourselves, and make it possible that, in future, other people can become free without bloodshed and bitterness." If he got drunk, and he didn't have much to do up here only get drunk, he'd say it over and over again, almost, I sometimes felt, as if he didn't really believe it himself. "I know there's those will misunderstand what I'm doing." '

There was a long pause.

'Were there?' asked Minnie.

'Oh ay. Sure enough.'

Kevin coughed.

'I suppose we really should go.' Minnie slipped from her stool. 'We mustn't keep you standing round all day.'

'I've seen great changes.' He tapped slowly out from behind the bar. He barely reached her eye level. So Uncle Frank, and then imperishable Ivy, would fade in front of her eyes, and then in the years to come she would herself.

'And not all of them for the best, either. So few people care for anything, only themselves. The young people can't wait to get away. What sort of a country have we made that people don't want to live in? Look at my own.'

Kevin went out into the hall.

'There's Bill Maguire down the road, stood up with the best of them, gun in hand, when it was needed. Eight over there, he has. Eight. There's no persuading them. This is just a place to come for the holidays. Bring the young ones over for a couple of weeks. Screaming round the place with their cockney accents, won't even bless themselves when they pass the chapel. If we'd visions and foresight, I suppose we'd never do anything. My heart was broke the day they murdered the Big Fellow.'

Minnie touched his arm. Outside in the hall, Kevin clinked the paint tins together.

'Don't go upsetting yourself, Big Jim.'

His voice took on a child's petulance.

'It's seeing yourself. That's what's got me all upset.'

They walked in silence towards the door.

'You'll be back to talk to me again?'

'I will indeed. In the next day or two.'

'Them Kellys want watching. They're a fearful crew.'

'I don't know what we'd do without them above.'

'Is that us you're talking about?'

Kevin came into the room again. He stood by the door, visibly impatient, waiting for Minnie to leave.

'Yes,' said Minnie, 'that's you.'

'Well, you won't have to put up with me for long. In spite of Big Jim's speeches I'll be away as soon as I've saved the fare. Mind you, that won't be today nor tomorrow. Bar digging a deep hole somewhere, there's no hiding money away from the old fella. If he's in need of a drink, or a skite, he'll pull the house apart until he finds some money. One day I'll do it, though, and then you won't see me for a puff of smoke.'

'God help England when the Kellys get there.' The old man wheezed with laughter. 'Or is it America you fancy?'

'England'll do me fine.'

They moved slowly to the hotel door. Minnie could see that Kevin had slung the three paint cans along the handlebars of her bike.

'Do you mind walking?' he asked.

She shook her head. The old man remained behind her in the hall.

'There's a couple of Yanks coming next week. Maguire. I mind Maguires up the hill at the back of you. Used to work for your granddaddy. I think it was to the States some of them went. The red Maguires they were called. There was a whole clatter of them once.'

'Are you coming, Minnie?'

'Yes.'

She turned to Big Jim and held out her hand.

'Goodbye, Big Jim. I'll be down again to see you, like I said.'

'Goodbye.'

The old man faded into the darkness, stick tapping on the lino.

By the time they reached the house again the clouds had blown together. The shy sun had gone for the day. The sky looked like an enormous unmade bed. At the yard gate the rain spilled down on them. Minnie ran across the yard, her feet splashing through the morning's puddles; Kevin followed pushing the bike, the cans swaying on the handlebars. By the time she reached the nearest stable door she was drenched. She held the door wide for Kevin with one hand, squeezing the water from the ends of her hair with the other. He propped the bike against the wall and swung the cans one by one down on to the cobbled floor.

'Gollee. What beastliness.'

'You get used to it.'

'What's the paint for?'

Kevin closed the door behind him. The cobwebbed window was a grey patch on the wall. He fished a cigarette out of his pocket and stuck it in his mouth.

'You might well ask. These walls.' He flicked a match alight as he nodded round at them. 'Damn useless walls, useless work.' He ducked his head down towards the flame. The cigarette caught. 'The Major likes the stables kept in order. Given a coat of paint every couple of years. Keep them up to the mark for the day he brings half a dozen thoroughbreds up from the Dublin Show.'

'What nonsense.'

Cobwebs clung to the wall, like morning mist to the fields. In the next stable someone scraped.

'Will you have a fag?'

He looked sombrely at the flickering match in his fingers.

'No thanks.'

He let it fall. Before it hit the floor the flame had burnt out. A small red worm lay for a moment near his foot. The scraping stopped.

'Don't you think it's nonsense?'

He shrugged.

'I do what I'm told.'

'Are you going to start now?'

'Tomorrow.'

'I'll give you a hand.'

'Don't bother.'

'Honestly, I'd like to.'

'Suit yourself.'

The indifference in his voice clawed at her.

'I've got to do something,' she mumbled. 'Can't sit up there all day sucking my pencil.'

He wasn't listening.

'Cormac!'

Boots clattered in the next stable. A door creaked. Cormac pushed the door open and stood, butt in fingers, in the grey gap.

'Did you call?'

'I thought you were going to have it finished for me.'

'It's all done but this.'

'All was what we said.'

'I'll finish it in the morning.'

'Today was when I wanted it.'

'Tomorrow's when you'll get it.'

For a moment Minnie thought Kevin was going to hit the boy, but he turned and let a kick out of him at one of the paint cans instead. The little boy was grey from head to foot, plaster and webs clinging to his hair and clothes. His eyes were red-rimmed, like a miner straight from the pit.

'Why don't you both come up and have a cup of tea?'

Her suggestion was ignored. Cormac took a long draw on the cigarette.

'He went out, just after youse left, and hasn't been back. I had to do the cows.'

'OK. OK.' Kevin turned towards Minnie. 'That'd be nice. How about the old one?'

'She won't mind.'

Kevin slicked back his hair with one hand. It looked as if it had been cut with a broken lawn-mower, no asset to a face, trying to curl, but not allowed, on Sundays lathered with reeking green oil, for the greater glory of God.

Cormac continued the argument. 'Youse took a queer long time, anyway. Would it be too much to ask what yiz were up to?'

He ducked away from Kevin's fist.

'None of your lip.'

'Do come on and have tea, if you're coming. I'm frozen.'

She went out into the yard. Over the trees by the drive the rooks were taking their evening exercise. The wind tossed them carelessly just above the branches. 'Soon it'll be spring,' she said to herself. Kevin's feet followed behind her.

'Lock up for me, before you come,' he called back over his shoulder. 'Do something for your wages.'

Minnie sighed. She thought of herself at fourteen, chewing ink-blue nails over her scientifically designed desk, the *Aeneid*, Book Four, dog-eared, illegally margin-noted, ablatives and datives dancing in front of her eyes. A ab asque coram de sine something pro and pre. The girl at the desk in front had a permanent wave and her brown hair lay on her neck in a tight Negroid fuzz. Unattractive. Pay attention. Don't dream. Could we have your whole mind on the problem please, young lady. Would you please stand up and tell the class what you find so interesting in the garden. Pius Aeneas, pater Anchises. Miss Fauldes had a gold link watch and two gold teeth, and as she leant towards you, urgent finger pointing at the meaningless words, her Swiss lawn, hand-embroidered blouse gaped and you could see her cold white breast neatly strapped away in satin underneath. Untouched by human hand. Her breath smelt of peppermints.

Miss Fauldes dissolved, and the flaking green of the kitchen door was in front of her nose.

'What did you say?'

She turned to Kevin, afraid he might have spoken.

'I never said a word.'

She put her finger on the latch and the door creaked open into the warmth.

'Don't be tracking mud into my kitchen.' Curls of potato skin fell from the gleaming knife into the sink. 'The tea is wet.'

She never turned her head, went scraping on. The two at the door bent to take off their boots.

'I've Kevin with me for a cup. We're both frozen.'

Ivy turned and stared at the two of them. 'How's your poor mother?'

'OK.'

Ivy sniffed disbelievingly. 'When's she due?'

Kevin shrugged and his face went red. 'I'm not sure.'

'A lot of interest you seem to take.'

'What do you want me to do? Stand on my head?'

Ivy turned back to the potatoes.

'Please God I won't be there when it arrives, anyway.'

He sat down at the table smoothing back his wet, gleaming hair with the palms of both hands. Might have owned the place, his toes sticking out of his socks towards the range.

'You're planning to leave.'

'And quick.'

He smiled with confidence at her broad back. She flipped the last potato into the pot and let the water out of the basin.

'That'll be one cross off your mother's back.'

Minnie took three flowered cups from the dresser and put them on the table.

'None for me,' said Ivy, her eyes on them as she turned round.

'Cormac,' explained Minnie.

Ivy moved heavily to the range, pot in hand. Metal clashed on metal. Drops of water sizzled on the stove.

'A fine time to be inviting Tom, Dick and Harry in for cups of tea and I in the middle of cooking the dinner. Are you sure you wouldn't like to bring your guests up into the drawing-room?'

The tea was chestnut-brown. Steam curled above the cups.

'Milk?'

He nodded. Minnie pushed the sugar bowl towards him and he

helped himself. Three heaped spoonfuls he stirred in. Pale china tea and lemon slices in Aunt Katharine's drawing-room. Silver spoons on transparent saucers. Soft powdered faces. His ten red fingers warmed themselves round the cup. His eyes stared at nothing through the steam. Minnie poured milk into her cup and sat down. Ivy, grumps strangely gone, bent down and opened the oven.

'. . . that's where I fell in love, when stars above came out to play . . . the mission bells told me . . .' The words died away. The smell of roasting meat filled the kitchen, and the sound of spitting fat, and Ivy's clock beating time on the shelf.

Cormac opened the door, and the dark wind blew him in, boots and all. He came across the floor and stood by Kevin's chair.

'Is all locked?'

'Ay.'

Minnie handed him his cup. 'Would you like some bread and butter?'

Cormac looked at Kevin, who shook his head sharply.

'No thanks,' said the boy.

'Sure?'

He nodded.

'They'll be having their tea when they go home. Good evening, Cormac. I never saw sight of your dadda the day.'

'He's away off,' said Kevin.

'Ay,' agreed Cormac, 'away off.'

Ivy turned from the stove and stared at the three under the white light.

'So you're thinking of going?'

'I am going,' corrected Kevin.

'I'm going, too,' said Cormac.

Kevin laughed. 'That's a good one.'

'England, I suppose?'

He nodded.

'I've told him he'll hate it. You honestly will, you know.'

'I'm going, too, so I am.'

'Not with me. Or running after me, neither. Amn't I trying to get free of the lot of you?'

He pushed his empty cup over the shining white American cloth, his eyes fixed on the red flower blooming gaily on the china.

'Me? Get free of me too?' He was wounded, voice and eyes, Minnie saw.

'Every one of you. You're on my back. This whole place is shoving me into the ground.'

He stood up and walked to the door, stockinged feet quiet on the flagstones. He stooped and pulled on his boots. When he straightened up his face was purple.

'Come on, Cormac. It's time we were home.'

'He hasn't finished his tea yet.'

Kevin jerked his head at the door. The boy put his cup down on the table and winked at Minnie.

'He's the boss.'

'So I see.'

'Will you come on!'

He pressed his finger on the latch and winter threw the door open, wind tearing through the room. He moved out into the darkness, Cormac scurrying after, his stunted shadow.

'What time are you starting in the morning?' shouted Minnie after them.

'Half eight.'

'I'll be there.'

The door banged. After a moment's silence, Minnie got up and piled the cups and saucers.

'Leave those. I've the sprouts to do.'

'It won't take a second.'

'Just leave them when you're told.'

'OK.'

Her fingers played with the edge of the table. Ivy creaked to the sink. 'On you go. Away up and get out of your wet clothes or we'll have you in bed, and I've no time to go carrying trays around.'

'They're nice boys, don't you think?'

'They could be worse, but you're not to go making free with them.'

'Such a load of old rubbish you talk.'

'Ttt. I've said my say, and if you pay no heed to me, I'll have to be lodging a complaint with the Major.'

'Ivy.'

Her hand was on the door knob. Beyond, the dark passages waited, sighing with impatience for footsteps, breathing, company.

'Away on up, now. My temper's rising.'

'You're an old dote and I love you like a mother, but you do get the snarls from time to time. Maybe it's the change of life.'

Ivy turned an outraged face towards the door, but Minnie was gone, skittering away, flicking down the light switches as she ran, muttering a prayer of gratitude to those in high places who had thought up rural electrification. What was worse than a dark passage? Two dark passages, a whole house full of dark passages, where shadows waited to sigh as you went past. The bulbs flowered into dusty light and the sighing stopped.

The Major arrived home as Minnie was drying her hair. Her housecoat (Harrods, five pounds bar a penny – she'd a lot to thank Aunt Katharine for, when you came down to brass tacks) touched her knobbly ankle bones. Bare feet. Slippers gone somewhere, leading a life of their own. Toenails needed cutting. A dreadful bore, but soon they'd be savaging holes in the toes of her shoes. She twirled her hair round in her fingers and held it up on top of her head. Looked sideways, frontways angled in the glass. Nineteen, if a day. No raving beauty. Pass in a crowd. Beauty is in the eye of the beholder. Alas, not really true. She let the hair fall down around her shoulders and attacked it with her comb, looking round behind her slightly nervously, remembering. Little bits of me are OK. Teeth. She bared her teeth. Good teeth. That's of little consequence, though, unless one wants to ensnare a dentist. How awful people look who smile all the time. Eyes. Low average. Too small. Mary Thompson Buchanan at school had eyes like a film star. Right bitch, anyway. Wearing size thirty-eight bra at the age of fourteen. A self-confessed slayer. Nothing in trousers could resist her. Suppose, just suppose, you spent all your life and nobody loved you and you loved nobody. Was it humanly possible, anyway, to love anyone more than you loved yourself? Saints, perhaps. The car lights flashed in the mirror, dazzling her for a moment. There he was, never known to be late for dinner. Below, in the hall, the bitch barked joyfully. The car door slammed and his old man's feet slurred on the steps. What was love, anyway? Nothing to do with Mary Thompson Buchanan and that sort of carry-on. Wasn't it something so big that the human frame couldn't contain it? We cut it down to our own mean little size all the time. Only saints. Greeting the dog, soothing with words and hands the heaving, stinking body. The boot-room door banged and the idolizer threw herself on the ground, nose to the gap, tail twitching. Minnie made a concerted effort to find her slippers.

She came down the stairs, fingers tipping the banisters, polished by two hundred years of grasping hands, skirt skimming the dying carpet. Hands clenched in pockets, below her the Major tramped across the hall, the bitch at his heels. At the dining-room he paused, barely a pause, put one hand against the lintel to steady himself as he manoeuvred into the room. Minnie ran down the last few steps and into the dining-room behind him. Ivy stood by the sideboard, her evening apron on. The Major had reached his chair, when Minnie threw an arm around his neck and kissed his cheek. He averted his head, and steadied himself with one hand on his chair.

'Uncle Proinnseas.'

'Ha.'

He sat down abruptly. His eyes flickered wildly from side to side. Then he pulled himself together.

'Good evening . . . ah . . . my dear. Ivy.'

Ivy dipped the ladle in the soup tureen.

'Evening, Major.'

'You were a thousand times mean not to bring me.'

'My dear girl,' he protested.

'What were you doing there, anyway?'

Sore, sad eyes, whites stained red, globs of mucus glittering in the corners.

'Ah . . . business. Yes. You would have been . . . Thank you, Ivy . . .'

He picked up his spoon and looked suspiciously at the soup she had placed in front of him.

' . . . bored.'

He tried a drop on his spoon, then scratched at the corner of his moustache.

'Eat it up. It's good and nourishing, and I don't cook good food to be left on plates.'

Ivy left the room, closing the door behind her. Minnie took a piece of bread and broke it into her own soup, a habit Aunt Katharine had strongly discouraged.

'I could have fiddled round.'

'Bloody awful rain all day.'

He tried the soup again, and then laid his spoon down with finality.

'Don't feel . . . Tiresome drive . . . Your stomach shrinks as you get older.' He excused himself.

'You're not ill, are you?'

Minnie looked at him anxiously. He shook his head. A lost tear wandered down one of the cracks in his cheek. He put up a finger and wiped it away.

'No. Whacked. Bloody awful rain. Roads like glass.'

'It cleared up here in the afternoon.'

'Ha.'

'I went down the village with Kevin to get the paint for the stables.'

There was a very long pause.

'Have to keep the stables up to the mark. The Show. Might get a couple . . .'

Two long minutes later he remembered her.

'Finished?'

She nodded. He groped with his foot under the table for his mother's bell. They heard it jangle in the kitchen passage.

'I'm going to give him a hand with the painting tomorrow.'

'What's that?'

'Kevin, a hand.'

'Splendid. Mustn't let the stables get run . . . Don't feel you have to.'

'It's not that. I'd like to. Now that it's settled,' she gave him a quick look, his face was vague – lost, really, the most lost face in the world, 'that I'm staying, I feel I must work out a plan for living.'

'Yes, of course.' His voice was polite, but it was quite impossible to know if he was listening or not. He pressed his knuckles against the cool wood of the table. The door opened and Ivy came in, dishes on the tray steaming, her face pink. The Major sat up straight.

'Well, Ivy. How have things been on the home front today?'

She sniffed at his soup plate as she removed it. 'Nothing changes. The house didn't burn down and the lough didn't flood. Kelly didn't turn up for work, but that's nothing new. A good thing it'll be, the day you get up in your senses and look for someone else. Are you up to carving?'

He waved a finger in her direction. 'Carry on.'

The knife squeaked as Ivy drove it through the meat, setting Minnie's teeth on edge.

'Hungry, Minnie?'

'Absolutely starvers.'

'That's what I like to hear. Day in, day out, cooking food for people who don't care what you put down in front of them. Don't eat more than a bird.'

'The older you get the less you want to eat. Need. Stomach . . .'

Ivy clattered a plate down in front of him.

' . . . shrinks. A medical fact.'

'Your stomach must be smaller than a fly's, for all you put into it.'

She left the room again, heading for her heaped waiting plate of potatoes and gravy. The Major took his knife and fork and pushed the food round his plate. Another tear rolled down his cheek.

'Uncle Frank . . . Uncle Frank.'

'Ha.'

'I had a chat with Big Jim Breslin today.'

He looked at her, puzzled.

'When we went down for the paint.'

'Ah, yes. The paint. Years since I last saw Big Jim. Years. Must be getting on now.'

'He seems to have been a great friend of . . .'

'Yes. He was.'

'He chatted a lot about him. It was very interesting.'

The Major pushed his plate away, couldn't stand the smell of it under his nose another second.

'One way or another, brother Pat spent more time than was good for him in the Pier Hotel. And money, I presume. I never enquired.'

'He talked a lot to Big Jim.'

'The trouble with this country, you'll find as you get older, is that people talk too much and do too little. Now I, as you may have noticed, do nothing, but at least I don't waste people's time by talking.'

He gave a nasty little laugh.

'But, Uncle Frank . . .'

He rose abruptly.

'If you'll excuse . . .'

He marched, the complete soldier, to the door, and then caught the handle the way a drowning man catches at a lifebelt. He swayed. For a moment she thought he was going to fall; then he turned, looking over her head at the dark corner of the room behind her.

'My brother, your father, was thought by some – or, ah, possibly, many – to be a charming man. Delightful. But he did nothing but damage. Smiling, drinking in public houses, debts, writing that ridiculous stuff in the papers about "workers, unite!". Biting the hand that fed him. Didn't even marry a girl he could bring into the house. Killed his mother. All the world lost was a smiling face when he died.'

He caught her eye, and his face went red. His fingers crawled over the brass handle. 'I'm sorry.'

She nodded.

'Bertie made something of himself.'

She nodded again.

'I didn't mean to upset you, about your . . . This place was falling apart when your grandfather died. No one could have expected me . . . Anyway. . .' He pulled open the door with a great effort. 'I suppose, when all's said and done, a smiling face is better than nothing.'

She nodded. He bowed towards her and left the room. She heard his feet crossing the hall. The boot-room door opened and closed.

Chapter Three

February 28.
The last few days have passed in a kind of mental turmoil. The more I see of the state of things here, the more I realize how hopeless things have become. Is it my problem? My father didn't seem to think that it was his. Are one's responsibilities towards others, or oneself? How do you ever find out in time to do the right thing? I hate my age. In spite of my expensive education I feel quite unfitted for life. There should be a pool of sensible, logical advisers to whom one can turn. Lean your head against their cool, stainless-steel chests and hear the soothing answers, the only answers, spoken in muted, unemotional voices. I have only my ghost, a trifle hysterical.

I worry about Uncle Proinnseas's health. For two days after his trip to Donegal he never appeared. Ivy, with a face of dignified resignation, carried trays to his room. She carried these down apparently untouched. She had the look of an early Christian martyr, and was best avoided, in case her simmering temper suddenly boiled over. However, he seems back to normal now, and amiable as usual, if you could ever call him amiable.

My novel is growing in my head, and I have numbered all the pages in a red notebook. I must try and find a typewriter somewhere. I'm sure it would have a splendid psychological effect.

The children of Lir come to life again today, after thousands of years of wandering. At the moment I am having a problem with their stepmother, Eva, who will keep turning into Aunt Katharine, who seems to lack the grandeur of real evil. A newspaper magnate, seeing endless possibilities in the four frail old creatures, takes them under his wing. Two doctors are in attendance night and day, wonder drugs in plastic containers always at hand. A public-relations man nurses them around the world, arranging television appearances, serial rights of their memoirs for glossy magazines, press conferences, personal appearances for charity. They are searching for the holy man with the Cross, and until they find him they know they cannot die. All too soon they are no longer news. They slip from the front page to the second, to a tiny sentence in a corner. The magnate calls off the doctors and the public-relations man, and they find themselves living in a slum in Paddington on National Assistance, and who the hell cares!

Looking at it like that, bare, black and white on the paper, it seems unlike what I have in my mind.

Then there's Kevin.

*   *   *

The paint ran back over the jutting bones of Minnie's wrist and her arm. The sleeve of her jumper was smeared with white. The brush stuck to her fingers.

Kevin, up the ladder, laughed. 'You'll never make a painter. It's lucky your life doesn't depend on it.'

'There must be a knack in it that I haven't got.'

'If I've told you once in the last two days, I've told you a thousand times: you put too much paint on the brush. Looka.'

He dipped his brush in the pot hanging from the ladder, touched it delicately against the side of the pot and then stroked it across the wall. No drips, no splatters, a neat line, merging unnoticeably with the rest of the painted wall. He looked at it with pride, then back down at Minnie.

'You want to use your wrist.'

She sighed.

Three loose boxes were nearly finished, and from the fourth and last they could hear the sound of Cormac scraping down the loose plaster and whistling as he worked. Minnie wiped her hands on a rag, and tried again.

'Do you like horses?'

'I can take them or leave them.'

He climbed down and moved the ladder several feet along the wall.

'Uncle Frank keeps saying he's going to buy a couple.'

Kevin laughed. 'That'll be the day.'

'I suppose he might.'

'Ah, be your age, Minnie. He hasn't enough cash to pay for the paint, let alone a couple of horses.'

'When he was young, he and Uncle Bertie used to hunt all over Ireland.'

'Sure, if the poor old man got on a horse now he'd only fall straight off and break his neck.'

Minnie's fingers were sticky again. She wiped them surreptitiously on the leg of her trousers.

'If you won the sweep, what would you do?'

'What do you think? Get out.'

'Even if you'd all that money? Would you not stay then?'

'I'd ring up Dublin for them to send me up a private plane, and I'd be gone before you could look round.'

'Then?'

He picked at a spot on the side of his nose. A tiny bubble of blood appeared.

'I'd buy a house like you see on the pictures. You know what I mean?' He spread his hands out illustrating stature, fine red brick and shining windows. 'With a swimming pool, you know, with chairs and tables all around it, and my own personal bathroom. Boiling water at the touch of the tap. I'd just hang around. Sit by the pool. Pals, drinks, everything that opens and shuts. Have a great old time till all the money was gone.'

'I don't believe you.'

'Why wouldn't you?'

'You'd have to do something. Everyone has to do something. Well . . . that's how it seems to me anyway.'

He laughed. Not a nice laugh.

'That's all you know. People like you always talk like that. The fellas with money always seem to think there's something wrong when the other fellas start wanting money.'

'I've no money,' she protested.

He looked at her with contempt. 'You know well what I mean.'

'Now you really are angry.'

'Yes.'

'We were only talking. Chatting.'

He sighed.

'It's the terrible need for money. The . . . the . . .' She watched him search desperately for the right word. He gave up. There was a moment's silence between them. 'I've got to get out or I'll die.'

'You do exaggerate so.'

'Tell you one thing.' He grinned. 'I'll not give one penny of it away. It'll all be for me.'

'Your deserving family?'

'Not a brass farthing.'

'Ah, Kevin.'

'No invites to stay either. None of them soiling the carpets.'

'Ah, now you're joking.'

'I don't make jokes.'

He watched her rub a sticky white streak on to her face with the back of her hand.

'At school they din into you to love God and Ireland and your mam and dad.' He paused, and in the silence drew another neat, white line on the wall. 'And of course the Virgin Mary.'

Cormac's whistling had stopped.

'Well, one thing I've learnt since I left school is they never gev me anything, nor never will, nor the likes of me.' His face was violent, almost, she thought sadly, like his father's. 'And I'll make damn sure I never give them anything either.'

In the next box something clattered to the floor.

'I'll not let them kick me around much longer.'

'How can you ever tell?'

He leant towards her.

'Money. I'll make enough money over there so they have to tip their hats to me. English and Irish alike. Call me "sir". I'll dazzle them with silver coins.'

She laughed.

'I'm glad to be amusing you.'

'I didn't mean to be rude. I was appreciating your use of words. I just don't think you know what's ahead of you, though.'

'I know what I want. Which is more than you know.'

'I'm working on it.'

'Will you come to the pictures with me one night?'

Minnie looked up at him, surprised. He painted away, face a trifle flushed, but apparently unconcerned about her reply.

'Seriously?'

'What do you mean, "seriously"? Of course seriously.'

'I'd like to very much.'

'Great.'

He climbed down and moved the ladder along to the last patch. He climbed up again.

'Nearly through.'

'Yes.'

'In ten years, you'll see, I'll have a cupboard full of shiny leather shoes. I read somewhere once that some film star had fifty pairs of shoes. I'll better him.'

'I like that. Will you come and take me walking?'

'Do you like to walk?'

'Yes.'

'I will so. You can have a special pass to get through the gate. No shot fired in your direction. Ssh.'

He held up the brush, stared sternly down at her, demanding her silence.

There was a clatter of feet next door, Mr Kelly's snarling voice; Cormac whined like a frightened puppy. Kevin laid the brush down on top of the can and climbed slowly down the ladder. He stood listening, head bent. Mr Kelly's words were inaudible to Minnie, but his voice had a hysterical sound. A sudden blow, and the sound of running feet. Kevin's face was still marble. The room darkened as Mr Kelly's figure filled the door.

'I'll teach the little cur who gives the orders round here, and you too, me bucko.'

I saw him hit a horse in the face once, Minnie suddenly remembered, punching it with his balled fist as if he'd like to kill it.

' "Cut the house wood", I told him.'

'It's too hard for him.'

'What was that?'

'You heard. I said I'd do it for him this afternoon. He'll only hurt himself with that axe.'

He took a step towards his son. Minnie moved. She didn't know where she was moving to, or why. Her foot hit the paint pot on the floor and slowly overturned it. A slow river of white spread on the floor.

'Oh.'

The man and the boy turned to look at her.

'You're more trouble than you're worth.'

Kevin bent down to pick up the pot and smiled into her face as he straightened up.

'I'm afraid I am.'

Mr Kelly's clenched fingers relaxed. He laughed nervously.

'I didn't see you, Miss Minnie.'

'I was just giving Kevin a hand with the painting.'

'Ivy was at me that there was no wood in the shed. The young lad shoulda done it. If he's old enough to take the Major's money, he's old enough to do a day's work.'

He leant towards her, his mouth smiling confidently, his eyes full of meanness and charm. She could smell the drink off him.

'They want all the good things of the earth, the young ones. To drop into their hands.'

He held his two hands out, cupped, waiting for a shower of gold. The nails were horny, brown, like an animal's claws.

'Wouldn't either of them do a hand's-turn, if I wasn't at their backs, night and day. It's like a disease. All over. Rotting the world.'

Kevin climbed the ladder again and continued with his work.

'We mustn't keep you from your work, Mr Kelly.'

He moved to the door, then turned, his face malicious.

'And the Major. I hear he's not too well after his trip to Donegal.'

Dirty voice. Brown tooth stumps, like decaying trees. She turned away, trying to ignore whatever he was trying to say, picked up the brush once more.

'He'd want to mind himself. Like the rest of us, he's not getting any younger. He'll need to take a bit of care.'

Who did she think she was, anyway, turning her back on him like that? Wasn't it common knowledge that Mr Pat married her

81

mother in a registry office in London, and the child three months on the way? What sort of a marriage was that, even for a Protestant? As good as a bastard, she was. His mind smiled sourly at the word. Bloody Maire Keating up the pole. Have to get shot of her before it showed. Pay her fare to England. One-way ticket. Pity. Money. A hot bit in her own way, too. Never mind, plenty more where she came from, always willing young ones growing up. Give herself another couple of years there and she wouldn't be too bad. Wouldn't have an eye for the likes of him though. Off after some fella on a horse, or an English eejit, with his pockets lined. Money. Must get Maire off before she causes trouble. Find some money somewhere. A few quid. Snivelling bitch. Kevin and Minnie painted on, apparently not noticing him at all. He pulled at his lip with two earth-grained fingers.

'I'll be off so.'

Neither of them answered him. He walked away. They waited until they could no longer hear his steps.

'You'd better get the turps and clean up that mess you made on the floor,' said Kevin.

'OK.'

'I'm away to confession.'

Ivy, buttoned into her serviceable navy best, velours hat to match, bought many years ago in Clerys, on a trip to Dublin, shoes ebony shining, stood in the drawing-room door. Minnie looked up from her exercise book.

'Mmm.'

'Did you hear me, anyway?'

'No,' admitted Minnie, 'sorry.'

'Ye've that look about you. I'm off now. To confession.'

'It's a terrible night to go anywhere.'

An army of savages battered at the windows.

'It's over a month. More. Must be near on two.'

'I can't believe you sin much. You must be hard pushed to find things to confess.'

'That's enough of your lip. A little bit of thought about your own sins would do you no harm.'

She left the room, and in a moment the hall door slammed behind her. There was no sound, only the wind fighting and crying in turn. The bitch, pressed against Minnie's feet for tangible company, opened her eyes and stared into the flames, seeing only her god's tormented face dancing in the smoke.

Minnie's head bent again over the book on her knee.

After a long time, the bitch's tail began to thump gently on the floor. She raised her head and gazed with expectation towards the door. Minnie leaned over and scratched her neck.

'There. Silly old thing.'

Shrugging off her hand, the bitch rose and moved across the room. Minnie looked up. Standing in the doorway was the Major. His sad, pale face poked out of the neck of the fawn dressing-gown that Aunt Katharine had bought him for Christmas. Minnie was glad to see that he wore it. His wrists were covered with black mittens. His hands drooped like dying flowers. The bitch, worn out by the walk across the room, sat down and lashed her tail from side to side. Minnie pushed her books behind her.

'Hello.'

'Ah.'

'I hope you're feeling better.'

'Fit as a . . .'

He came into the room, closing the door behind him.

'Fiddle. Yes.'

He came slowly over and sat down in his chair.

'A fiddle.'

He stared absently at her. The bitch arranged herself happily against his feet.

'Minnie. Ha.'

He could feel his chilblains beginning to heat up already. His fingers twitched.

'Can I get you anything? A cup of coffee or something?'

He shook his head. They stared at each other in silence.

'Ivy's gone to confession.'

'Ah.'

'It's a terrible night to go all that way.'

'Ah.'

'I suppose you could call it a sort of penance in itself.'

The Major cleared his throat. 'Ha. Ha.'

'It's nice to see you down again.'

'And you. What have you been up to?'

He suddenly seemed his old self again. Snuggled his thin bottom into the chair and stretched his feet out towards the fire.

'I've been helping Kevin paint the stables.'

Her uncle looked surprised.

'You remember. I told you the other night.'

'Oh. Ah.'

'It honestly seems an awful waste of time.'

'What's that?'

'A terrible waste of time. When there are no horses.'

'Spring Show coming up any time now. Might take a trip down to Dublin. Stir my old bones. Good for me. Put a new bit of life into me to get out of this place for a while. Several things I ought to do down there. Look up a few old friends. See the doctor. Haven't been feeling quite . . . not quite . . . lately. Check up. Probably buy a couple of hunters. Get back in the swim again.'

He leant his head against the back of his chair and laughed like a boy. 'Haven't been on a horse for donkey's years. Make a bloody fool of myself. Have to take a few lessons. Like a kid. Learn all over again. Instinct. Once learnt, never forgotten.'

Exhausted, he closed his eyes. Hooves drummed in his ears. Baying. The creak and jingle of harness. Panting. Sweet winding sound of the horn. Thundering. Nothing but men and horses moving over the green, under the tumbling clouds. Baying. Thundering. Sharp, crackled orders. Hooves thundering. Guns. Baying and the scream of shells. Sweet winding sound of horn and scream. Hounds, black, tan and white, tearing and snarling. Broken bodies on the green. Dead eyes staring at the tumbling clouds.

'You're always saying you're going to buy some horses.'

'What?'

His hands. Oh God, his hands. His nails clawed.

'You're always saying that you're going to buy some horses. And you never do.'

He felt the accusation in her voice.

'This time I . . . You'll see. Must get back in the swim. Feel as fit as a . . .'

'Well, until such a moment . . .' She paused, searching for the right way to put it. '. . . wouldn't it be a good idea to make use of the stables?'

He blinked at her.

'With profit in view.'

'I don't quite see . . .'

'Deep litter hens or something. They wouldn't be any trouble. I could look after them. The library has books about them. There's always a market for eggs.'

'Out of the question.'

She sighed.

'I mean to say, what a ridiculous suggestion, when I've just told you I'll be putting a couple of hunters in there in six weeks or so. What will you do with your whatsit hens then?'

She didn't reply.

'Hey?'

'I don't know.'

'Ha.'

He looked triumphant. A general who had just won a decisive battle. Angrily, Minnie pulled the notebook out from behind her and began to write again. Her hair made a curtain between them. He pulled a paperback out of his pocket and put it on his knee. Who did she think she was, anyway, teaching him his business? Fooling around with hens. I suppose the money for hens comes out of the air. Snap your fingers and bingo. He snapped his fingers. The bitch looked up expectantly. Minnie pushed the mess of hair out of her eyes and looked over at him. He felt he should say something.

'What's that you're writing, anyway?'

'A novel.'

He smiled politely. 'What?'

'A novel. Do you think that's terribly silly?'

'Taking after your father?'

'He never wrote a novel, did he?'

'Couldn't say. All I know is he never wrote anything that brought him in any money. Bolshevik rubbish in the newspapers.'

'I don't have any ambition to become a journalist.'

'Ha.' He flipped the pages of the book on his knee with a finger. 'Have you ever read anything by Dostoievsky?'

'Certainly. *Brothers*, you know . . . years ago. Only read trash now. As you get old . . . Of course, I have.'

'Do you think there's any possibility that I could ever write like him?'

'I'd say the chances were remote.'

He picked up the book and looked at a word or two. She sighed.

'Young . . .' he said, looking at her. He paused for a very long time.

'Yes?'

'Young people think they know so much about things. In reality, they know nothing.'

'I've read a huge pile of books since I came home.'

'Indigestion.' He raised the book up between them. 'Anyway, if you're going to be a writer, you don't want to waste your time looking after hens.'

'There's loads of time for everything.'

He sighed and began to read, forgetting her.

Chapter Four

I find it impossible to commit to paper my feelings about Kevin, though, as each day goes by, I find them harder to ignore. I detest the ignominy of blushing when I hear his voice in the yard. I despise myself for hoping that approaching footsteps will always be his. Ivy suspects, and glares around her like a lioness who scents danger. She constantly hints and probes with dart-sharp words my tender conscience. I am cute as a fox and evade all. I won't be drawn. I won't commit. But still, in spite of all, she knows. My only fear is that she will tell Uncle Frank, and he will be compelled to take steps.

* * *

The Major, fully dressed, Guards tie neatly knotted, the regulation distance below the Adam's apple, every inch a squire, looked with distaste at the letters by his plate. Only one in a white envelope. Didn't know the writing. Thank God it wasn't Katharine again, anyway. More lectures about the child. He picked it up and slowly carried it to within an inch of his eyes. The writing curled and uncurled on the paper like a hundred tiny snakes. Ridiculous state of. Must see eye man. Things going from bad to. The writhing stopped and the words lay neat and clear below his eyes. He picked up his knife and slit the envelope cleanly along the top. Minnie crunched ridiculous breakfast food, staring at, but not seeing, her paternal great-grandmother simpering at her from the wall. Large-eyed children and ecstatic animals leaped and posed gracefully round her billowing skirts. Blue Irish mountains curved in the background under a blue Irish sky. Minnie saw nothing. Corn flakes scrunched between her teeth. The triangles of toast in the silver rack were already cold.

'Ha.'

Minnie looked at him. His voice was angry. He took a sup of his scalding tea, and, as he let it trickle gently down his throat, he re-read the note in his fingers. Pester, pester, pester. If it wasn't Katharine, or bills, or the bloody government, it was something else. Why could nobody ever leave you alone? He threw the letter down on to the table and chewed at the corner of his moustache.

'Ha.'

He felt Minnie's eye on him. 'Yes. Some impossible American fellow wants to come up and see me. Some crazy notion about his grandfather having worked here.'

'Must be the Maguires.'

The Major looked at the letter in his hand. 'That's the name, all right. How did you . . .'

'Big Jim mentioned them. They're staying at his place. The red Maguires, he said they used to be called.'

'I presume the adjective applied to the colour of their hair, rather than their politics.' He sighed, and searched back through the junk-room of his mind. 'I don't recall anyone of that name.'

'Of Kilaclooney.'

'Kilaclooney.'

'Above the bog.'

'Yes.' His voice was irritable. 'Yes, yes.'

He picked up the *Irish Times* and arranged it to his liking against the teapot. Minnie reached out for a piece of toast. Somehow

Aunt Katharine's toast was always hot. More appetizing.

'Kilaclooney. Hasn't been a soul up there for over forty years. All upped and gone somewhere.'

A black-coated politician smiled genially at him from the front page of the paper. Rapscallions, rascals, crooks, every one of them. Jumped-up sons of grocers. Kilaclooney. He leaned forward, the better to catch the small black words. A dazzle of sunshine danced on the flailing picks as six of his father's men ripped the roof off a cottage. He watched silently from the trap. His governess had let the reins go slack and the pony cropped the grass. The brass trappings glittered. A lark's whirling song faded above them. The name of that particular governess eluded him. He only remembered sandy eyelashes that blinked with each axe blow. Hunks of greying thatch slithered into what had been someone's living-room, bedroom, kitchen. Beams cracked like the gunshots of later years. Bertie pulled a paper bag out of his pocket and shoved a sweet into his mouth.

'Can I have one?'

Slowly Bertie folded the bag and put it back in his pocket.

'You have your own.'

'I left them at home.'

'Too bad for you.'

A bed and a couple of chairs stood on the turf. Among the small crowd of watchers, a woman cried.

'Greedy pig.'

'Beggarman. Always cadging. Bet you've eaten yours already.'

'I have not.'

'Have so.'

'Don't fight, boys.'

The governess picked up the reins and flapped them against the pony's back. For a long way down the hill they could still hear the thudding axes.

'Your father's been too kind to them for too long.'

She took the whip from its leather holder and flicked the pony lightly. He twitched his ears and began to trot.

'Give these people an inch and they'll take an ell. They refuse to understand that he has to live, too.'

The lark whirled down towards them again, unconcerned with anything but its own song.

'Hail to thee, blythe spirit,' said the governess.

Must be well over fifty years.

'Bird thou never . . .'

'What?' asked Minnie.

'Hah, I sometimes wonder why they bother to come back.'

'Mmm.'

'Flash their dollars around. I suppose since they've asked we'd better have them up for a cup of tea.'

'That would be very nice of you.'

He bent towards the paper again, trying to collect his thoughts. His napkin-covered finger poked at the corner of his right eye, digging out the early morning crust.

'Tomorrow. Sunday. Most suitable.'

He sighed with relief, the decision was made.

'OK.'

'Your presence would be . . . ah . . .'

'Desirable?'

'Exactly. I'll, ah, scribble a note, if you would . . .'

'Of course.'

*   *   *

'Come in, girl, come in.'

Big Jim called to her from his chair beside the window in the bar.

'Come on over here beside me and let me get a good look at you.

I knew you'd be back before too long to have a chat with me.'

He seemed to have grown even smaller in the few days since she'd seen him. Looked like a grotesque doll propped in the chair, an untidy bundle of newspapers tucked down beside him.

'I've a note for Mr Maguire.'

'The Major'll see them?'

Minnie nodded.

'That'll please them. Give the note here to me and I'll put it into the gentleman's hand myself. Don't be rushing away on me. Pull up a chair. The girl has the kettle on. You'll have a cup of tea?'

He waved at her to sit down.

'You'll have to excuse me not getting up. The legs are queer and bad today. Maire,' he screamed, in a high, cracked voice, 'bring another cup when you're coming.'

'Is that really all right?'

'Of course it is. I'd offer you a drink because you're your daddy's daughter, only you're under age. They have a car from here to the end of the street. Silver decorations sprinkled all over it.'

'The Americans?'

'Surely. A great pair. Rich beyond all. Generous with it. He's forever handing out the cigars. A great one for a laugh.'

A dark girl wearing an apron came out from the kitchen with a tray. She put it down on the table between them and smiled at Minnie.

'It's only made. Give it a couple of minutes to draw.'

'Thank you. That's gorgeous,' said Minnie.

'And now she wants to go to America, too,' grumbled the old man.

'Why wouldn't I? Everyone says it's a great place.'

'You never gave it a thought till you saw them and their car.'

'You've no notion what I gave a thought to and what I didn't.'

'Isn't your own country good enough for you?'

'Who's there in this place to appreciate my finer qualities?' She turned to Minnie. 'Passage paid and fifteen a week they're offering.'

'It sounds marvellous.'

'I'd be a fool not to take it.'

'I suppose so. You can always come back.'

'Back, is it? You'll see me back in me own good time. You'll get the itch yourself one day and there'll be no holding you.'

'Well, I don't know what I'm going to do without her in this place. She's the only one with her head screwed on at all.'

'Thanks for the compliment. I'll give you my custom when I come back in my sheffewer driven Rollses Royce.'

'You could at least wait till I die.'

'And be here till doomsday. I've bread in the oven.'

She turned and left them, practising her sexy American walk across the bar.

Big Jim watched her with a certain wistful appreciation, until the door swung shut. He turned to Minnie.

'How are things above? Pour out you. I couldn't lift the pot today, with the way the old hands are. Four good spoonfuls. The wife, God rest her, used to say I liked tea in my sugar.'

His chuckle turned into a cough, and the cough into a paroxysm. One gnarled fist beat helplessly at his chest. Minnie wondered whether to call the girl back, but he gestured at her to get on with her tea and not mind him. Gradually the fit passed over and he stared at her, pain in his eyes.

'Every night I pray to the Mother of God to let it be my last. But they won't let me go.'

She didn't know what to say.

'Have a drink of tea. It'll sooth your throat.'

'It's ironical,' he smiled over the rim of his cup at her, 'in the end of all, even I want to leave the country.'

She laughed awkwardly at his joke, not really wanting to, but afraid he might be offended if she didn't. He pulled himself together.

'As I said before, how are things above?'

'OK, I suppose, Uncle Frank hasn't been too well.'

'I heard tell.'

'He seems better today. I wonder should he not see a doctor. But it's a difficult subject to broach. He tends not to like interference.'

'Doctor how are ya.'

'I find him hard to . . . hard . . . I really can't work out whether he hates me being there or not.'

'A close man.'

'Yes.'

'I wouldn't worry your head. It's your home. You have a right.'

'I suppose so.'

'He was a fine young man. Great on a horse. It's strange he never married. He had a great mind to go to Africa after the nineteen-eighteen war, but the old man wouldn't let him.'

'Why ever not?'

'You never asked the old man for reasons. You did what you were told. Only Pat had the courage to say "boo" to him.'

'I'm glad he was a man of spirit.'

Big Jim cackled. 'Spirits is right. "Never open a bottle," he used to say, "without throwing away the cork. One of the major rules of life."'

'I didn't mean that.'

'I know ye didn't, girl. I'll tell you something. A little story about the first time your daddy impinged himself into my life.'

He snuggled himself back into his chair pleasurably, and the papers by his side crackled.

'The night it was that we burned the lodge.'

'Our lodge?'

'Sure enough. There was a great old wind blowing straight down the lough. The waves were lashing over the wall here and drowning the houses. Never seen anything like it before or since. Anyway, up went the lodge, like putting a match to a heap of dry grass, and the wind so loud we nearly couldn't hear the screams of your man inside in his bed, when he realized what was going on.'

'You didn't let him burn to death?'

'Divil a bit. Let him get to the door in his nightshirt and then shot him in his tracks.'

'Big Jim, how awful.'

'He had it coming to him. Don't waste your tears. One of our own he was. Turned informer. A quick death was too good for him.'

He took a long drink of tea and thought about it. 'Ay, too bloody good.'

'You're being a bit gruey.'

'It's life. He was a Judas. Nothing's too bad a death for the likes of him. It's always on my mind it was treachery killed the greatest man among them all. I'll never forget that. Let you not forget it, either.'

'No,' said Minnie, not quite sure who he was talking about.

'There we were, anyway.' He snuggled his tired bones further and further down into the chair, till she thought he'd disappear altogether. 'Ten-thirty in the pitch dark, watching the leaping flames, and the sparks streaming away like army banners in the wind. Covered we were after from head to foot with a thousand smuts.'

'And the man lying dead in the doorway?'

'For sure. Better that, than roasting inside.' He tittered. 'I bet he's roasted ever since. Anyway, at the height of the conflagration, who should come around the corner but your granddaddy and the Major. Just the two of them, sitting up straight on their horses like military men. Toy soldiers that you'd buy in a shop. The old man's face black as the night was in it. "What's going on here?" shouts himself. The Major was carefully behind him; I think he thought we were going to shoot down the both of them out of hand. "We've just executed a traitor, sir," answered our commandant, cool as you like, "I advise you to get back on up to the house and mind your business, this is a military operation." "Military operation, my backside!" yelled your man. "Might I enquire what right you have to go murdering people on my land?" A few shuffles, a few coughs from the lads. I believe that, left to ourselves, we'd have run, every man of us. "May I remind you, sir, that there is a war being carried on in this country," says the commandant, real cool. "If that's what you like to call this ridiculous carry-on, that's your affair. I prefer to call it thuggery, and I refuse to be intimidated into condoning murders on my own land. I warn you here and now that I have called the police, and I'll see every man jack of you up before the courts on a murder charge. And don't think I can't recognize you behind those dirty handkerchiefs." Then Tom Slattery loses his head entirely and lets a shout out of him. "Will I kill him, sir?" "Ye'll do no such damn fool thing," said the commandant. In the silence after, we heard the ominous sound of the Major cocking his pistol.

' "One move out of any of you scallywags and the Major'll blow your brains out." We hardly dared breathe, knowing the Major for a nervy class of a man. Then, suddenly, out of the air, from up behind the Major's head came a great shout: "Up the Republic. God save Ireland and death to all supporters of the Crown!" The old man nearly fell off his horse with rage.'

'My father.'

'The very fella. The commandant shone his torch up into the trees and there he was, not a day over ten, grinning from ear to ear. We all burst out laughing. Delighted with his reception, didn't your man pull a tricolour out from under his coat and wave it in the air! In the confusion that followed, with the old man and your uncle trying to get the young lad down from the tree, we melted, as you might say, into the darkness, and were home in our beds, with our allybys, by the time the police arrived. I gather your granddaddy near skinned the boy after, such a rage he was in.'

'And the dead man?'

'The what?'

'The body, the dead man. What happened?'

'We just left the mortal remains to toast. I think your grandfather had him buried after.'

'Tell me one thing, Big Jim.'

'I will if I can.'

'Do you think I should go and live in England with Uncle Bertie?'

'What would you want to do that for?'

She didn't reply. He looked her over thoughtfully and sighed.

'You're the spitting image of your daddy, sitting there pondering on things. The week before he was killed, wasn't he sitting there reading a letter from the Major saying if he ever put foot in the village again he'd have him jailed.'

'Good Lord. Why?'

'He got wind of a plot was in Pat's mind. Like I said before, there's traitors everywhere, and Pat was always one for shooting off his mouth. He had some notion of the people rising, loys and pitchforks in their hands, and taking over the old place, which they would then run for the common good; he kept saying things like: "from each according to his ability, to each according to his need." He had a great old gift of the gab, but most people thought it was easier in the long run to go to England to earn their living. Anyway, the Major and the priest run him out of the place. First time the pair of them were ever on the same team.' His head nodded down towards his chest. Tired eyes closed momentarily. 'Them old airioplanes is desperate things altogether.'

'Under the circumstances, it was pretty good of Uncle Frank to take me in.'

'People do odd things for odd reasons. Not a single survivor, the papers said. You take your life in your hands when you go up in the sky like that. Only scattered wreckage on a mountainside. Here one minute, gone the next.'

'Things are safer nowadays.'

'Maybe. He'd a deal more spirit in him than my own son. You might say he lived till he died, and there's not many you can say that about. I pray every night for death, but he lays his hands on others.'

'You're a bit depressed today. You'll feel better later.'

She stood up. The chair legs skrawked, like angry chickens, on the lino.

'No. I'll never feel better. I hardly even sleep now. The days seem like weeks. It's patience I lack. God grant me patience. He's better things to do than listen to the moanings of an old man.'

'I'd better be off.'

'Yes.'

'Thank you for the cup of tea.'

'You'll be back, won't you?'

'Of course I'll be back.'

He raised a claw, and then dropped it on the table, and seemed to be asleep.

'Goodbye,' she whispered and tiptoed out.

'Stop.'

Kevin leaped out of the ditch right into her path, the flat of his earth-grimed hand up, facing her. She put on her brake and balanced herself with one toe touching the road.

'Hello.'

'Hello, yourself.'

He brought his hand down on to the handlebar, grinned sheepishly at her.

'I've been waiting. I saw you go down the road. You've been a queer long time.'

'I was talking to Big Jim.'

'More likely he was talking to you.'

'He's so lonely.'

'He's a bloody old bore.'

She got down from the bike and he took it from her and wheeled it towards the ditch. He let it drop against the hedge. Winter grey twigs snapped under the weight.

'Hey.'

'I had to get out of that place, or I'd've gone mad. He's fighting drunk. Laying into anyone gets in his light.'

'Shouldn't he be working?'

Kevin laughed. 'I'd a thought you'd have noticed by now. He works when he wants to.'

'Yes.'

'It's a pity the Major doesn't notice.'

'I suppose he does, really, but he can't be bothered.'

'It's a great day.'

Cold as charity, but great whale clouds swimming in the sky.

'The winter's nearly gone.'

'I thought we might go up the hill.'

'We?'

'Yes. You and . . .'

'You?'

He nodded.

'Who else?'

'I'd miss lunch.'

'It's up to you.'

He looked indifferent. She thought of Ivy's angry face. Lips tightly zipped together. Words thrown like handfuls of sharp pebbles. Sticks and stones will break my bones, but words will never kill me. Uncle Proinnseas will never even notice. He can't be bothered. What was one lunch missed, not going to make a habit of it. The hens would benefit. He broke the silence, his voice startling her.

'Where's the harm, anyway?'

'OK.'

He reached out and patted her shoulder, surprising himself as well as her by the gesture.

They turned off the road up a boreen. The cart ruts were filled with water, and here and there reflected the blue from above. A silver plane droned in seemingly pointless circles. Water sang and splashed in the ditches. The smell of turf smoke curled round a bend in the lane, and a dog drooped towards them to sniff their legs. In the crook of the curve a cottage stared at them malevolently with tiny black eyes, and a small child repeated the stare with her blue eyes and one finger stuck in her nose. A few white rags were thrown across the hedge to dry, and half a dozen hens pecked at nothing on the road.

'Shoo.'

Kevin waved his arms, and they screeched in all directions. The dog growled softly. The child stared. Round the bend the hedges ended and the boreen became a track between low stone walls. Mountainy sheep with strong legs for climbing were scattered among the whin bushes, which seemed to flower with little tufts of grey wool. The skeleton of a car sat in a field above the cottage, an old Austin Seven, anything of value gone. The wind suddenly blew sharply in their faces, carrying the smell of distant rain.

They walked in silence. Kevin, with an unlit cigarette dangling from the corner of his mouth, stared at the ground just in front of his feet.

'You're not very chatty.'

'No.'

'What's up?'

He shrugged and walked faster. She had almost to run, to keep up with him.

'You wouldn't understand.'

'Why did you ask me to come if you were just going to be grumpy?'

'I didn't want to be on my own.'

'You're walking too fast for me.'

He slowed down a bit.

'I once did a terrible thing. It's often on my mind.'

She waited silently for him to continue. For a long time it looked as if he wasn't going to. Then he spoke, hurriedly, like someone about to dash off and catch a train.

'I've never told a soul. Not a soul.'

He turned his head suddenly and stared at her. She nodded.

'It's always in my head. Nothing I do makes any difference. Sunday a fortnight ago I was coming back from the dance. Cycling down the main road about twelve or so, and I seen something. A form in the ditch. The left-hand ditch. I got down from the bike to have a look. It was my father. Lying there as if he was dead, only he was snoring and dribbling like a lunatic. He hadn't been home for four days. I felt in his pockets to see if he'd any money, but he hadn't, and I knew he was on the way back to us.'

She nodded to show she was listening. It didn't matter, though, he was talking to the air.

'There's never anything for him to do but come home when the money's gone. Anyway, I took a hold of his legs and pulled him out of the ditch. He only groaned a bit. And I pulled him into the middle of the road, and then got on my bike and pedalled away, leaving him laying there, in the hopes that a car would have come along and run over him and I'd never see him alive again. Did you ever do that? Did you ever think of such a thing? Trying to kill someone. Then do you know what I did? I turned round after a half a mile and pedalled back again. He hadn't stirred. I took him by the heels and threw him back in the ditch again. I hadn't the nerve.'

He groped in his pocket and pulled out a box of matches and lit his cigarette. He took a long pull on it.

'I can't help wishing all the time that I'd a had the nerve.'

'It's just as lucky you didn't.' Just for the sake of saying something.

'No one would ever have known.'

'You.'

'If only I'd a had the nerve. And her too. I hate her, too. Dirty tinker, snivelling in the corners, never sticking up for us. Letting him beat the daylights out of her, and then lying quiet in the bed and letting him make babies on her whenever he can't find anyone else to play his dirty games with. Babies nobody wants, and who don't want to be born.'

'You shouldn't say things like that.'

'I knew you'd never understand.'

'I don't have any parents . . .'

'It's well for you.'

'. . . what I mean is that I've no one really to love or hate. I feel detached.'

He looked blankly at her.

'I mean, I can see my uncles calmly. No strong feelings. Not killing sort of feelings.' She paused. Inside her head she knew what she wanted to say, but the words that stumbled through her lips were wrong. The blind leading the blind.

He laughed suddenly, 'You're only a kid yet.'

'Yes,' she agreed.

'Come on so, kiddo. Race you to the top.'

He was away off up the track, like one of the mountainy sheep with a dog on its tail. Minnie followed at her speed. No walls now on either side, the path wound steeply up round rocks and whins and clumps of heather drab without the purple flowers. The wind strengthened and she had to brace herself to stop being whirled down the hillside again. Below, in its nest of trees the house stood, smoke twirling from three of its many chimneys.

Lunch was on the table. The Major played with his knife and fork, pretending to eat. The electric fire scorched the leg of her empty chair. The Major's eyes crossed and re-crossed the pages of his book; fingers scratched spasmodically at the burning chilblains. Ivy gave out to the air.

The plane droned above, and a pillar of rain blew up the lough. The moving finger writes.

'Nice trouble you'll be in when you get home.'

'Oh God, not you again.'

'Manners.'

Minnie shrugged.

'And it's all in aid of what?'

'I didn't come up to scratch. He wanted something, and I wasn't able to give it.'

'Pardon me if I smile.'

'Go ahead. Laugh your silly head off.'

'There's only one thing men want from women, or to be more accurate in your case, boys want from girls.'

'That's a lot of ballyhoo.'

'Wait and see. I suppose you think you're cute, anyway. Following in Father's footsteps. Forming an attachment for a social inferior.'

'You really are disgusting.'

'A peasant.'

'You forget. I'm half peasant, as you call it, myself. I just like him. That's all. Like.'

'Don't think those sex shivers have escaped me.'

'My own affair. I can cope.'

Laughter.

'How about going to England?'

'Do shut up and go away.'

'London. The centre of the world. Uncle Bertie'd greet you with open arms. His little colleen.'

'No.'

'What you don't realize is that there's no need for you to become an English lady. On the contrary. Cultivate your brogue. Destroy them with your uninhibited wit. Blarney them up. You want to be a writer. How about a vitriolic lady columnist? Or a writer of daring TV plays for the over-twelves? There are openings everywhere.'

'Give over.'

'Your daddy was a failure. He never grasped the essential fact, there's no cause like your own cause. He wasn't the hero you fondly imagine him to have been. Just a seedy failure. Go to England.'

'When I want your advice I'll ask for it. Now kindly go away. I have an assignation at the top of this hill.'

'You can't get rid of a good ghost like that.'

'In nomine . . .'

'Haa-haa-ha. You'll kill me with laughing. That sort of carry-on's quite out of date. There's just one last point I must mention before I go.'

'What's that?'

'Don't you notice that your companion smells? Stinks. Bad breath. Arm pits. Unwashed clothes. Ugh.'

Like a child, Minnie put her fingers in her ears.

'I'm not listening,' she said loudly.

Laughter. Fading faintly on the wind.

'Probably even got nits in his hair.'

A whisper. Silence.

Minnie ran up the last rise. Clouds banked up across the sky, swallowing the sun momentarily. A circular patch of turf, surrounded by rocks, and wind-flattened bushes, made the top of the hill. Kevin lay curled in the shelter of one of the rocks and waved to her as she appeared. He had taken off his jacket and spread it beside him on the ground. He patted it with his hand. She ran over and threw herself down beside him.

'Gosh, I'm dead.'

There was no wind where they lay, and a gentle warmth came from his body, like heat from a stone on a sunny day.

'You've been long enough!'

'I was just taking my own time.'

She lay down, and they stared into each other's faces, till Minnie turned suddenly away and transferred her stare to the sky.

'It's going to rain.'

'Not for a while yet.'

'With luck.'

'You didn't mind what I said earlier?'

'Why should I mind?'

'I don't know what came over me to tell you.'

'You can say anything to me. We're friends. I'll never mind anything you say to me. I know you think I'm only a kid, but we really are friends, aren't we?'

He put out his hand and touched hers.

'I was only pulling your leg.'

They lay in contented silence for a long time. The clouds covered the sun for longer and longer periods, and they began to feel cold.

'How much money have you saved?'

'Just enough to take you to the pictures tomorrow night.'

'No. Jokes apart.'

'I'm telling you no joke. I had near on ten pounds hidden in a box. I don't know when he found it, but I went to put another pound in yesterday, and I found the lot gone, box and all.'

'Are you sure it was your father?'

'Of course. It's not the first time. He's a divil to hide money from. He smells it out. I think he even has Mam on the lookout for him.'

'Oh Kevin, I'm so sorry.'

'We'll spend the whole bloody pound tomorrow, and then I'll start from scratch again.'

'If you give me the money I'll mind it for you.'

He shook his head. 'No, thanks.'

'No? Why not?'

'I wouldn't like you to get mixed up in all this. He wouldn't give a damn who he caused trouble for.'

She sat up, hugged her knees to her chest with long chilly arms. 'I've been thinking.'

'Mmm.'

'Maybe it's crazy, but I've had an idea. You know the garden.'

'Of course.'

'It must have been a super garden.'

'Once upon a time. In the good old days.'

His voice was ironic.

'Well, why shouldn't we get it into shape again? Get rid of all that mess. Grow vegetables. To sell, I mean. I'm sure we could do a deal with some of the local hotels. You know, plant something slightly more original than cabbages. Don't you think all those fruit trees could be rescued? If I could lay my hands on sixty or seventy pounds it would give us a start.'

'If, if, if, if.'

'What do you think of the idea? I could pay you to help me, and when it gets going we could be partners.'

'You're out of your chinese. Don't you know I'm going to England?'

'You don't have to. Just listen to me a while.'

'How do you think the Major'll take it?'

'He'll never know until it starts to work. I won't tell him.'

'He'd be sure to find out.'

'How? He never goes out of the house these days, and if he does, it's only to make mysterious trips in the Ford. I'd pay you enough to get yourself a room in the village.' She looked anxiously at him. 'I couldn't begin to do it on my own. But I'm sure the two of us . . .'

'Where were you planning to get the money?'

'I hadn't really thought that far. Perhaps Uncle Bertie would help. Once we got going we could move on to something else. Employ people. Get the whole place back on its feet. Gradually.'

'You've got fine big ideas.'

'Why not?'

He got up, and walked over to the edge of the hollow and looked down at the countryside below. She saw him brace himself against the wind.

'Come here,' he called to her over his shoulder. She went over to where he stood staring down at a group of cottages crouched below them, roofless, black-eyed, tired of standing. Three flat-topped pines lamented over them.

'Kilaclooney,' said Minnie.

A voice was blown up to them by the wind.

'Someone's there.'

'Maybe it's the Americans Big Jim was talking about.'

'Ay. You're right. There's their car below.'

He pointed to the road curling in the distance and she saw the gleaming monster. They both suddenly began to laugh.

'Imagine,' Kevin waved his hands towards it, 'coming all that way . . .'

'In that Cadillac, Pontiac, Chevrolet or whatever . . .'

'. . . three thousand miles or more . . .'

'. . . to visit your ancestral home. Headquarters of Clan Maguire . . .'

'. . . and find . . .'

'Oh hallelujah, ever been had.'

The sun was gone for good. The grey clouds were so low now on the hills, that you felt you only had to stretch up a hand to burrow it into their woolly softness. Their laughter died away, suddenly as it had come.

'We'd better get on down.'

She nodded. 'I suppose so.'

'It would all be so great if we could stay up here and never go back down to them.'

'Eating grass, and watching the scenery changing all around us.'

'Build a great big fire at night that could be seen blazing for miles around.'

'And by ships at sea.'

She put her arm through his and squeezed it against her side. He allowed the liberty.

'It would be no good, they'd only come and get us.'

A fat raindrop burst on her face.

'We'll have to run or we'll be drenched.'

'I hope the Yanks have their macs. Here, give me your hand, the path is slippery.'

Halfway down the hill he spoke again.

'Tell you what.'

'What?'

'I'll stay.'

'Kevin.'

The radiance of her face alarmed him.

'Hold on a minute. Don't lose your head. There's one thing . . .'

'Yes?'

'Get the money. Here, into your hand, and show it to me. Not a promise, mind you. Cash. Notes. Coins.'

'Chink, chink.'

He opened her hand and tapped the palm of it with a finger.

'Chink, chink. I'll give you a month. If you haven't got it by then, I'm away.'

'I'll get it. I swear I'll have it by then.'

Chapter Five

I've sat for hours, staring at the clean, cream paper. Gortnaree House, Co. Donegal engraved in the top right-hand corner, a relic of better days, no envelopes left since a long time. How do you ask someone for money? So much money. I see Aunt Katharine's forbidding face in front of my eyes the whole time. Hear the angry words dropping from her lips. 'Ridiculous. Out of the question. Mustn't encourage. Enough commitments of our own. Outrageous. Must come over here at once. Learn to earn her own living. Can't have a second Patrick in the family. Outrageous. Over here. At once. Now. Write to Frank. Ridiculous child.'

I'll have to try though. There seems no other way. Perhaps he won't show her the letter. Just unclip the Parker from his pocket and open his cheque book. 'God bless you, my child, in your venture . . . Saving the old place.' Unlikely. Terribly unlikely, let's face it. A sentimental scrawl. 'Don't worry your pretty head about turnips and cabbages, come back instead to your old uncle who needs you. Don't be upset about the whole terrible mess, and here's a fiver to buy yourself some extravagant thing to remind you of your loving uncle Bertie.' The cream paper is still clean, and I must go down in my high heels and pour out tea for the American pilgrims.

The Major paced nervously round the drawing-room, fidgeting

his father's watch in and out of his pocket, snapping it open every few minutes and peering down at the hands. Never been to the menders once in sixty years. Nothing was made to last any longer. Shoddy, catchpenny jobs. Here this year, gone the next. If you'd the money, buy another; if not, go without. He visualized a stream of shining coins pouring into the bottomless pockets of thousands of smiling manufacturers. The chimney blew out a puff of yellow smoke. Bloody birds again; must get Kelly to root them out. Ridiculous, anyway, when you thought of all the unused chimneys, and they had to choose this one to build their infernal nests. Damn. The smoke caught at his throat and made him cough. How much longer were these people going to keep him waiting? Incivility. He peered at his watch again. Just on four. Awful bloody bore, hanging around like this, when he might have been . . . what? Getting on with things. Fixing up his affairs. Hell of a lot of letters he was behind with. Have a few words with Kelly. Must keep him up to the mark. Endless jobs. Nobody ever realized just how much . . . He dabbed at his eyes with a khaki handkerchief. Bloody smoke. Ivy had really gone to town. He hadn't seen the Liverpool cups for years. Must be worth some money, those. Too many of them cracked, crashed in and out of basins by idiot maids with red, clumsy hands. Mother had loved them. Drank her *thé au citron* every afternoon on the dot of four, pale white fingers gently holding the gilded handle, transparent slivers of brown bread, faintly nut-flavoured. Oh, God. Best silver teapot out, too, dazzling. Think it was the President of the United States himself, instead of two pestilential tourists covered, no doubt, with photographic equipment. Please God they won't stay long. Bound to ask all sorts of questions no one can answer.

'Damn the smoke. The whole room . . .'

'It's the draught. I'll open the window a bit.'

'. . . stinks.'

Minnie opened the bottom of the window, and a piercing wind rushed into the room.

'We can either be cold and smokeless, or warm and choked. Take your pick.'

'It's the birds, in the chimney again.'

'I think it's the draught.'

'Must get Kelly up on the roof. Have a good look. Clear the infernal nests away.'

'Honestly, Uncle Frank, it's the draught.'

The Major sat down in his chair and picked up the *Observer* which lay on the floor where he had dropped it ten minutes before. Behind it he quivered with anger. As if he didn't know. Ever since he could remember, birds had been getting into those chimneys. Upstairs you could hear them banging around under the roof. In those days it was no problem. Nothing was a problem, somebody dealt with things like that. Smoke. Bloody smoke. Eyes agony. Burn them out, exterminate them. Get rid of the rooks, too, if it was possible. Appalling racket they made at six in the morning. Waken the dead. Not that he was ever asleep. Insomnia. Suffered for years. Must have a break. Change one's way of life. Out and about, see old friends.

'Shut the window, child. What's the point in lighting a fire, if you keep opening the windows?'

Without a word, Minnie closed the window. Another ball of smoke rolled slowly out of the fireplace. The Major threw the paper down on the ground again and got to his feet.

'Why do people have to keep pestering me like this? Wasting my time. Can't stand people. Never yet met an American that I liked. Katharine.'

'Aunt Katharine's not an American.'

'English people are just as bad.'

'Why don't you sit down quietly and read the paper?'

'How can I concentrate with these people just about to arrive?'
He snapped the watch open again and looked at it.
'Ten past. If I'm to have tea at all I like to have it at four.'
He sat down again angrily and picked at his moustache.
'You're a right old misery today. Aren't you feeling well?'
'I simply prefer to be left alone.'
'You never see a soul from one year's end to the next. It can't be good for you.'
'It's for me to decide what's . . .'
'Here they are.'
A shining black limousine swung its way into view, white-wall tyres and silver hubs sending the mud flying like sea spray in all directions. Minnie drew back from the window. The Major stood up and then sat down again. A nasal laugh, and the doors slammed discreetly. Feet on the steps, and then the distant jangle of the bell jumping on its spring in the kitchen passage.
Minnie moved towards the door.
'No,' said the Major, 'let Ivy.'
Minnie sat down on the edge of the sofa. The bitch raised her head from the hearth rug and stared at the door with interest; at the sound of Ivy's feet crossing the hall her head drooped down into sleep once more.
'Mr and Mrs Maguire.'
Ivy flung the door open.
'Major, sir,' she added, standing back to let the visitors past her.
Minnie and the Major jumped to their feet.
'Ha.'
The Major moved towards the Maguires, trembling hand out towards them.
The American gripped it in his own two paws. Sleek black hairs covered his wrists and the backs of his hands. He's really a bear, thought Minnie. Poor Uncle Proinnseas, death awaits you.

'Hi there, Major. Great to meet you.'

His two hands pumped. Minnie thought her uncle's fragile arm would break.

'Ah – great,' grunted the Major, struggling to get free.

'Allow me to present Lydia. Mrs Maguire.'

He let go of the Major and swept an arm in his wife's direction. Lydia, sensibly dressed for the occasion in a full-length mink coat, her arms heavy with jangling bracelets, slid her hand into the Major's.

'Charmed.'

She opened her eyes wide and smiled up at him.

He ducked his head in a strange little bow. For a moment Minnie got the impression that he was going to kiss the lady's hand, but he dropped the idea, and her fingers in mid-air.

'How do you do?'

'I'm just fine, thanks. We're both just fine, actually.'

He looked at her with surprise and then gestured towards Minnie.

'My niece. Ah . . .'

'Hi, honey.'

'Minnie.'

'Hello.'

A cloud of yellow smoke hovered dangerously near their heads. The Major waved a hand helplessly, trying to dissipate it.

'Won't you sit down,' suggested Minnie. They all moved towards the chairs.

'Is this your . . . ah . . . first visit to these parts?' the Major asked Mrs Maguire.

She settled herself into the corner of the sofa, cuddling her mink around her.

'Our first and, if I have my way, our last.'

'Aw, come on now, honey. She's done nothing but complain since we put foot in Ireland. I don't know what's gotten into her.'

The Major smiled politely.

'Now, darling, you mustn't give the Major the impression that it's only Ireland I find disagreeable. It's all of Europe. Do you know, Major – in all our long trip the only place I've really felt at home was in Switzerland.'

'Ha.'

'It's really cute. Do you know Switzerland at all?'

'Well, really . . . I can't remember . . . I don't . . . It's all so long ago . . .'

'You should take a trip there sometime, if you've never been. Like I said, it's real cute. Isn't it, Henry?'

Mr Maguire opened his mouth.

'He's such a bore about Europe. Of course, Ireland in particular. Fortunately my ancestors came from the other side of the Iron Curtain. You know, the wrong side. Way back, of course. So even if I wanted to, which I don't, I wouldn't be able to go and search for their tombstones.'

She flashed a huge toothpaste smile at the Major.

'They always told me the Irish were the most sentimental people in the world. I didn't believe them until I married one. I simply can't understand what anyone can find to be sentimental over in this country.'

'Aw, honey . . .'

'After all, the past's the past. Here we are, citizens of the greatest country in the world, what's the point in brooding about the past? That's what I say. Don't let the past bug you.'

'Yes,' said the Major.

'I'll tell you something. If I was President of Europe, or whatever, the first thing I'd do would be to pull down all those dirty old buildings and build new ones. Have you ever been to Italy?'

'I . . .'

'Well, take my advice and don't go. You know something?

I didn't even dare drink the Coke there.'

'Honey . . .'

'As for Ireland, I couldn't make him see reason at all. He simply insisted on coming. Simply insisted. And what do we find when we get to his ancestral home?'

She stared angrily round at them all. Minnie blushed. The Major, despair in his eyes, pulled at his moustache and cleared his throat.

'A heap of old stones. I nearly died. All that discomfort he's put me through, the cold, the food, the dirt.' Her voice rose to a semi-scream. 'Just so that he could come and gawp at a pile of old stones.'

'I took a lot of pictures.'

'I'll say you did. Kept me standing round for half an hour in the cold while you went click click with your camera. Honestly, you wouldn't believe it, he photographed that pile of stones from a thousand different angles. Tell you something, though. Those ones we don't show our friends. Imagine sitting watching their faces while Henry tells them that his ancestors used to live in that old pile of stones. Why, even in its heyday it can't have been much better than a cattle shed. No siree.'

There was a long pause.

'Switzerland is clean. No poverty. One thing I hate to see is poverty when I look out the window.'

'Quite,' said the Major.

The door opened and Ivy came in with the tea.

'Ah, tea,' said the Major.

'How can yiz sit in all this smoke?'

Ivy deposited the teapot and the hot water jug on the tray and creaked to the window in her Sunday shoes. She threw it open and flapped the smoke out with her hands.

'Amn't I forever telling you that when the wind is in the east this chimbly smokes unless you have the window open. Only a fraction, though. How many times have I told you that?'

She glared accusingly at Minnie.

'Never pays the slightest attention, that one, to anything you might tell her. Might as well talk to the wall. That's youth all over.'

She closed the windows down to the regulation fraction.

'It's the birds,' muttered the Major.

She turned on him.

'Now don't you start. Haven't I run this house for twenty odd years? And wouldn't it be a queer thing if I didn't know what was wrong with the chimbly. It's the east wind is on it. A little hat on top is what is needed. Many's the time I've told you that, but it goes in one ear and out the other. Men,' she fixed her eye on Lydia, 'are all the same.'

'Hahahaha.'

'That's a nice bit of fur you're wearing.'

'Ivy!'

'What would it be, now?'

'Mink,' said the lady visitor, with certain pride.

'Well, isn't that nice now.' Ivy headed for the door. 'It's a queer long time since there's been mink having tea in our drawing-room.' At the door she turned and addressed herself to Mr Maguire. 'It's great to think there's a Maguire from Kilaclooney able to buy a mink for his wife. God is good.'

She left the room; Minnie's nails scraped at her wrist to keep her from giggling.

'Minnie, will you pour out the ah . . .'

'Milk and sugar for you, Mrs Maguire?'

'. . . tea?'

'Only a touch of milk, please. I find the milk here very strong. I don't know what it reminds me of.'

'Milk?' suggested Minnie, passing her the cup.

'Whatever it is, it doesn't suit my constitution.'

'Milk and sugar for you, Mr Maguire?'

'No tea for me, thanks. Never drink tea.'

Minnie looked at her uncle. He frowned at the floor.

'Is there anything else I could get you?'

'There isn't a drop of drink in the place. Not a . . .'

'Don't worry your head about me, honey. I'm fine.'

'. . . drop. Not a drop.'

His tongue licked at the corner of his moustache.

'Don't worry your head, Major. He's under doctor's orders.'

'Nothing serious, I hope,' said the Major politely.

'He's been ordered right off liquids. A pint a day at the outside.'

'Ttt.'

'It may not sound difficult, but just you try it. Especially if, like my old man there, you're fond of your booze. He had a terrible weight problem. You should have seen him six months ago. Isn't that right, Henry?' She leant towards her husband and punched him fairly playfully in the stomach. 'Sixty pounds he's lost.'

'Ttt.'

'We'd started to plan this trip, but our doctor said he couldn't let Henry out of his sight unless he lost a whole lot of weight. He was scared his heart might just go – bam! It was a lot of hard work, but we made it. You feel a new man, don't you, Henry?'

'Sure do.'

'Do you know, Major, six months ago he couldn't even get round a golf course. Got palpitations when climbing the stairs. I was worried sick. I just insisted that he go and see our doctor, and not a moment too soon. He told me that if I hadn't brought Henry to see him when I did, he wouldn't have lasted more than another couple of months.'

'Dear me,' said the Major.

She put a hand on his knee.

'You're so cute. I just love the way British people say things like "dear me" all the time.'

She gave his knee-cap a squeeze.

'Well, you don't suffer from overweight, anyway. What a pity we can't let you have a little of Henry's surplus.'

'Ha.'

'More tea, Mrs Maguire?'

'No thanks, honey. One cup's plenty for me. Henry, I think you should broach our business with the Major.'

The Major rose, clearing the mucus from one side of his throat to the other, and brought his cup over to Minnie for a refill. Mrs Maguire smiled charmingly up at him.

'We've a little proposition. Go ahead, Henry.'

She settled herself snugly into her corner and waited for Henry to get on with whatever it was. The Major looked courteously puzzled. Remained standing, back to the fire, the cup trembling in his left hand.

'Go right ahead,' she menaced.

'Well, you see, we've just built this house for ourselves . . .'

'Almost a mansion, you might call it.'

'. . . just on the edge of Peoria . . .'

'The best side.'

'It's been two years building, you know what with workmen and plumbers and . . .'

'Henry.'

' . . . Anyway, it's finished now.'

'Electronic kitchen, three baths, closed-circuit TV, and a rumpus room.'

'I . . . ah . . . hardly see . . .'

'If Henry would get to the point.'

'A moment, Major, a moment; I am coming to the crux.'

Mrs Maguire turned to Minnie.

'We have every facility for projecting films in the rumpus room, and a hi-fi, colour TV, and a complete range of indoor sports . . .'

'I cannot talk against you, sweetheart.'

His voice was cold as the east wind. The voice that had got him his three-bathroomed mansion on the best side of Peoria. She turned up the collar of her mink, and sank her angry face down into it.

'The point is, Major, I wondered if you'd be interested in selling us your gates.'

'What? My what?'

'Your gates. I reckon this is what Lydia would term another instance of Irish sentimentality. You may or may not remember that my great-grandfather made those gates. They've always been a sort of legend in my family. You can't imagine the pleasure it would give me to be able to bring them back and hang them in our yard. Unlike my great-grandfather, I'm a rich man. I can afford to pay for my pleasures.'

There was an ominous silence. The Major put his teacup down on the tray and took his handkerchief out of his pocket. He wiped his mouth slowly.

'Am I to understand that you want to buy my . . . ah . . .'

'I reckon I won't be mean about it.'

'We'd paint them up, a bit,' said Lydia. 'Real cute, they'd look.'

'. . . gates?'

'That's it, Major. I won't beat about the bush. Two hundred dollars I'll give you for them.'

'Absolutely ridiculous.'

'Three hundred would be the highest I would go.'

'It'll cost a lot to ship them home, won't it, Henry?'

'My gates.'

'That's the idea.'

'It's not as if you used them,' said Lydia helpfully. 'We had a good look at them on our way here. They haven't been touched for years.'

'Preposterous.'

His face took on an alarming violet colour. Minnie trembled for everyone. The Americans seemed not to notice. Her mink eyelashes fluttered hopefully, like butterflies' wings.

'You don't have to worry about anything. I'll have a man sent up from the village to take them down. No trouble for you at all.'

The Major held out his hand to Mrs Maguire, who ignored it. He swung round and handed it to Mr Maguire, who shook it tentatively.

'Done?'

'If you'll excuse me, I have business to attend to. Minnie will see you out.'

'What about . . . ?'

'Goodbye.'

He bowed stiffly towards them and moved towards the door.

'But Major . . .'

He was gone down the passage, the bitch at his heels. The boot-room door creaked and banged. Minnie crouched back in her chair, hoping that no one would notice her.

'Well, I'll be damned.'

'He seemed such a sweet old boy.' Mrs Maguire stared at the door. 'Perhaps he'll come back.'

'No,' said Minnie. 'He won't come back.'

They turned round and looked at her.

'I hope we haven't upset the Major.'

Mr Maguire got to his feet. He took a cigar out of his pocket, bit the end off it, and spat it, with unerring aim, into the fireplace.

'He's moody sometimes.'

'Noorotic?'

'I don't know exactly.'

'Come on then, honey. No point in sticking around here. Let's get back to the hotel.'

'For hotel, read hell-hole.'

She got up and took Minnie's hand.

'Thanks for the tea, honey.'

'That's OK. Don't give it another thought.'

They moved out into the hall and Minnie opened the door. A gust of wind drove into the hall and the carpet rippled in small waves round their feet. They stood in silence for a moment as Mrs Maguire adjusted her coat, then Mr Maguire took Minnie's elbow and squeezed it thoughtfully.

'We'll be at the hotel for another couple of days . . .'

'Not if I can help it.'

'For another couple of days. Just in case the old boy changes his mind.'

'I'll tell him.'

'Do that. I reckon maybe, on reflection, the money might come in handy.'

His fingers flickered up her arm and then relaxed.

'Well, so long.'

'Goodbye. Goodbye, Mrs Maguire.'

'Goodbye.'

She watched them climb into their car and whisper off down the drive. The rooks were having their evening stint, hurling themselves round in the air.

'Of all the bloody cheek,' she said aloud, as she closed the door.

* * *

'So you see, it was all molto horrifico.' She peered through the dark at Kevin, who was stooped, chaining their bikes together against the harbour wall. She giggled.

'Awful, I mean. Only awful.'

She was glad she'd kept her heels on. His hair shone with oil, and somebody's navy suit neither fitted nor suited him. Ivy caught her at the door as she was leaving.

'Where are you off to in that get-up?'

'Flickers.'

'Come again.'

'The pictures.'

'Alone?'

'I must fly or I'll be late.'

'Alone?'

'With Kevin.'

She had slammed the door and rushed down the steps, not waiting to hear Ivy's undoubtedly acid comment.

Kevin straightened up and put the key in his pocket. As he moved, she got a whiff of the oil on his hair, and felt inclined to laugh. His face was red from stooping. He wore a red vee-necked pullover under his suit, and a tightly knotted tie.

'What did the Major say when they'd gone?'

He took her arm and guided her across the road, around the shining puddles. Not too far away red lights wrote 'Roxy' in the darkness.

'He just disappeared into the boot-room and never came out again.'

'The boot-room?'

'Yes.'

'Why?'

His fingers were warm round her wrist, barely touching, but comfortable. She hardly dared move her arm in case he took his hand away.

'What does he do in the boot-room? What is the boot-room, anyway?'

'It's where all his hunting gear is kept. I don't know any more than that. I've never been in there.'

'Never?'

'It's his very private spot. Sanctum sanctorum. I don't know what he does in there. I think he'd be raging if I went in to see.'

'It's odd to think there's a room in your house you've never been into.'

'There's heaps of rooms I never go near. No one has for years. Ten empty bedrooms, untouched by human hand in my memory. You open a door and the smell of damp makes you feel ill. Beastly Victorian wallpaper is bubbling off the walls. Ugh. Spooky.'

'We could move in and you'd never notice us.'

She didn't laugh. He took his hand off her arm and swung away from her, over towards the wall, rattling some loose coins in his pocket.

'Upstairs or downstairs?'

'I don't mind.'

'We'd better go upstairs.'

That was where the class went, reserved their seats by telephone, only hopping in at the last moment in time to see the big film.

'OK.'

She didn't sound as if she appreciated the jump he had just taken, from being a downstairs patron, to being an upstairs one. He wondered if he should buy some chocolate.

'How much did you say the Yanks offered for the gates?'

'Three hundred dollars. That's a hundred pounds, about.'

He whistled. A small figure lurched out towards them from the doorway, fag drooping from mouth.

'Hello.'

'Hello, yourself.'

'I'm coming wit yez.'

Kevin didn't answer. He took Minnie's arm again and speeded up.

'Come on. Pay no heed to him and he'll go away.'

Cormac's steps pattered after them.

'I have the money. You can't stop me going to the pictures if I have the money. Can you now?'

Kevin gritted his teeth and walked even faster.

'I can't walk that fast in my heels,' complained Minnie gently.

'Sorry.'

He slowed down abruptly.

'Going anywhere with you seems to be a series of races.'

'I've said I'm sorry.'

Cormac pulled at his coat.

'Can you? Can you stop me?'

'No, I can't,' said Kevin angrily. 'I just wish you'd bloody well leave me alone.'

'You always take me to the pictures with you.'

'Well can't you see, I'm not taking you this time?'

'Ah, let him come, Kevin. Where's the harm?'

'I don't have to take him everywhere I go, do I? Anyway . . .'

He looked at her helplessly.

'Are yiz lovebirds? Is that it? Ye want to be alone? Puh-puh-puh.'

He made little kissing noises with his lips.

'I'll bloody well kill you when I get home.'

Kevin began to hurry again.

'Puh-puh-puh.'

Several boys were leaning by the sweetshop window watching the talent going by. One of them nodded at Kevin, and stared with interest at Minnie.

'Puh-puh-puh.'

The coloured stills indicated covered wagons, Indians, cowboys, blazing guns and the exquisite singing of flying arrows.

'Puh-puh-puh.'

Kevin headed for the box office. Minnie stopped and turned to Cormac. She took her purse out of her pocket.

'Will you take a sixpence and stop annoying your brother?'

The lady cashier put aside the maroon sock she was knitting. Cormac grinned and spat the butt out on to the ground. His eyes fixed on her fingers groping in her purse.

'Ninepence?'

The lady cashier pressed the appropriate buttons and two half-dollar tickets flew out of their slot towards Kevin.

'Puh-puh-puh.'

'Aw, come on, Minnie, can't you. Pay no attention to the little get.'

'Here, go and buy yourself some cigarettes.'

She blushed as she held out a shilling towards him. Kevin took a menacing step in his brother's direction. Cormac grabbed the coin from Minnie's hand and was off into the darkness.

'You shouldn't have done that. What he really needs is a good kick up the backside.'

'Protection money. A sort of insurance against trouble. Gangsters all over the world make a lot of money that way.'

'I don't imagine that Cormac knows the rules.'

The cinema smelt of Jeyes Fluid and orange peel. The lights were dimming as they went in and the girl with the flashlight showed them to the front row of the balcony. The seats were warm, newly vacated.

'Here.' He shoved a bar of chocolate into her hand as the titles began to flash on to the screen.

The film followed its appointed course. The arrows sang, the guns crackled, a hundred hooves thundered across the sunlit scrub, covered wagons swung, with the beat of the music, into their defensive ring.

'Puh-puh-puh.'

Little jets of smoke puffed between them from the seat behind.

'Why don't you put your arm round her, give her a bit of an old cuddle?' Spoken in a hoarse and carrying stage whisper.

Kevin turned round and gave a clip at his brother with the flat of his hand.

'And there's more where that came from.'

There was silence from then on.

'I'm sorry about Cormac,' said Kevin, as they linked each other down the road towards the pier.

'All kids are the same. They like mickey-taking.'

'Will we leave the bikes and go home over the rocks?'

'I'd only ruin my shoes.'

He looked down at them. 'Yes.'

They reached the bikes and he bent down to unlock them.

'They're nice.'

'What?'

'Your shoes.'

'Thanks. My aunt bought them for me in London. She bought me a whole load of things.'

'Great.'

'Her generosity is loaded. She keeps thinking that if she tidies me up a bit, and shoves me into the London social whirl, some ghastly chinless wonder will lose his head and marry me.'

'Rich, though?'

'Oh, undoubtedly rich. That's the whole point of the operation.'

'Mightn't be a bad idea, so.'

'Oh, for God's sake.'

They went spinning through the puddles, up the hill, turn right and past the Protestant church. The rectory still had an upstairs light burning. Mr Coffey reading Agatha Christie in bed, thought Minnie, three pillows wedged between him and the headboard, the Bible on the bedside table, just in hand's reach. That was the last light. There wasn't even a moon. The darkness was intense and gusty damp.

'I've been thinking,' said Kevin.

'Mmm?'

'About that money.'

'What money?'

'The gates.'

'Oh, yes. That.'

'The Major must be a real thicko not to take it.'

'I suppose he has a right to refuse to sell his gates if he wants to.'

'Yes. But . . . A hundred pounds, you said.'

'About that.'

'Just what you need.'

'There's no point in looking at it from that angle. He'd never have given it to me, anyway.'

'Have you ever seen a ten-pound note?'

'No.'

'A fiver?'

'Seen them lots of times, but never owned one.'

'Just imagine having ten ten-pound notes.'

His hand crept to his breast pocket, as if they were already there, bulging out his pocket, crisp and new, crackling, like burning wood, to the touch.

'Or twenty five-pound notes,' she suggested.

'A hundred pound notes.' Neatly stacked in a small suitcase.

'Two hundred ten-bob notes.'

'Two thousand shillings.'

'Gollee.'

She began to laugh, and the light from her lamp swung from side to side on the road in front. A car came up behind them and they drew right over against the ditch. For a moment, their shadows jumped in front of them, then there was a shower of mud, blacker darkness than before, and the red dot in front growing smaller and smaller.

'I'm soaked,' grumbled Minnie, steering out on to the crown of the road again.

'Do you not think he'll change his mind?'

'Uncle Frank? Absolutely no. He won't even regret his decision.'

'Look, Minnie.'

'What?'

'Could we not do it ourselves?'

'Do what?'

'Take down the gates and sell them.'

'Honestly, Kevin. What a suggestion.'

'He'd never know.'

'It's stealing.'

'Not a bit of it. They're as much your gates as his. I bet he never gives them a passing glance. It's not as if you wanted the money for yourself.'

'It's out of the question.'

'It just seemed like a miracle to me.'

'Nothing doing.'

'Where else do you think you'll get a hundred quid?'

'I don't know. But I will.'

'It's not as if they were doing anyone any good, just hanging there, mouldering.'

'Shut up, Kevin. I said no.'

'Well, I'll tell you one thing; I'm not hanging round all my life waiting.'

She gritted her teeth so as not to yell at him.

'I appreciate your position.'

Into their silence came the sound of running feet, gasping for breath, sobbing, and there was Cormac grabbing for the handlebars of Kevin's bike. Kevin swerved angrily to avoid his hands, pushing his feet down harder on the pedals. In the dim light from their lamps, Minnie saw the little boy's face. She put on her brakes.

'Kevin.'

Kevin dragged one toe along the ground and gradually stopped. They peered at Cormac, who stood there between them trying to push words from his mouth towards them.

'What's up?'

'Mam.'

'Mam?'

'I think he's killed her.'

Without waiting to hear another word, Kevin was away into the darkness. The sound of the spinning wheels faded. Minnie threw her bike into the ditch and took Cormac's arm. She took a handkerchief from her coat pocket and handed it to him. He wiped his face and then kept it clutched in his fist.

'What happened?'

They moved slowly along the road, arm in arm.

'I thought ye would never come.'

'It'll be OK. You just wait and see.'

'I think he's killed her this time.'

'Nonsense. What happened, anyway?'

'I got back to find them at it.'

'Fighting?'

'Yelling and screaming at each other. And then she did a terrible thing. I saw her through the door. She put up her nails, like a cat, and scratched him down the side of the face. Drew blood. So then . . .'

'So then?'

'He punched her and punched her, and she fell on the floor and he went on punching her, and all the kids were screaming.'

'Oh, dear.'

'He never saw me. I just ran away.'

'I'm sure it'll be all right. Kevin will be there by now.'

'Kevin's no match for him.'

The door of the cottage was open and a strip of yellow-green light lay across the road. A child cried.

'That's Baba,' said Cormac.

He pulled free from Minnie's arm and ran to the door. Minnie followed slowly, reluctantly. Her London heels were filled with lead. Kevin stooped over his mother, a shadowy heap on the floor, her head covered hopelessly by skinny sticks of arms. The children stood around as close as they dared come, and stared. In the light from the oil lamp, their faces looked green.

'Mam.'

He put his hand on her shoulder. A long groan burst from under her arms. She seemed to want to push herself further into the floor to get away from them all. The baby screamed.

'Ssh-ssh, now,' said the girl who was holding it.

'Mam, are you all right?'

The floor below her was sticky and dark.

'Shouldn't you get the doctor?' whispered Minnie, afraid to speak aloud.

His green face peered up at her for a moment, placing her in his mind. He nodded brusquely. 'Maureen went to fetch him. Here, will you give me a hand to turn her over?'

Minnie stepped into the room. She only wanted to be at home, her books, her bed turned back by Ivy, nightdress folded on the pillow, her pens and notebooks on the table, waiting. Smoke and fear, and the sour smell of poor people, made her eyes run.

'I don't think you should move her till the doctor comes. There may be something broken.'

The woman whined, like a beaten dog. Minnie and Kevin knelt, one each side of her, and looked at each other helplessly.

'I don't want to touch her. I'm sure I'll throw up if I have to touch her. I want to run.'

'Ha-ha-ha. Life in the raw.'

Everyone seemed to be waiting for her to do something.

'Get up and run, then, if that's what you want. It's not your problem.'

She put out her unwilling hand.

'See, this is what comes of getting mixed up with the working classes.'

She touched the cold thin shoulder.

'Brave little Minnie soldiers on.'

She heard her own voice speaking. 'It's going to be all right.'

She had an idiotic feeling that the more you said it, the more likely it was to be true. She looked up at the children.

'Can't you put the little ones to bed or something? I'm sure they shouldn't be here.'

The girl with the baby in her arms shook her head. 'He's in there.'

'Dada?'

She nodded.

'Leave him, though.'

'This time I'll swing for him.' He stood up.

'Leave him, Kevin.'

'I'll leave him dead.'

'Will you so?' Mr Kelly stooped in through the door from the back room. 'Let's see you try.'

He moved slowly towards his son, keeping his balance carefully.

'Open your big mouth and say that again, and see what you get.'

Kevin avoided his father's eye and looked at the heap on the floor. 'You've near killed her this time.'

'And what'll you do about it, me bucko?'

He lifted his hand with surprising speed and slapped his son hard across the face. Kevin staggered slightly, and his eyes flickered with fear. His father's face burst open in a huge laugh.

'Go on,' he said gently, as if he was afraid of disturbing the woman on the floor. 'Hit me. Hit me, me brave boy, and see what I'll do to you.' The red mark of his hand lay on Kevin's cheek, like writing on a wall. 'Just the once. A little tap. I'm waiting to tear you limb from limb.'

He raised a booted foot and kicked the body on the floor. The woman moaned, but didn't stir.

'Oh, no, please,' whispered Minnie. No one heard her.

Father and son stared at each other.

'Brave boy.'

Mr Kelly moved a step away, as if he had forgotten what was between them. Minnie could see he was just daring Kevin to move. The children had gone. The baby still cried, only in the other room. Neither man nor boy was conscious of her presence.

'Our Father which art in Heaven, don't let Kevin touch him. Hold his arm, merciful Father.'

With a smile, Mr Kelly turned his back on Kevin and staggered slightly towards the smouldering fire.

'Dear, sweet, merciful Father, I'll never ask you for anything again . . .'

Kevin sprang.

'Kevin!'

Mr Kelly had his huge hands round his son's throat and was squeezing and shaking, like a washerwoman wringing out clothes. Minnie ran across the floor and took a hold of his arm.

'Don't, please!'

Mr Kelly looked at her. He threw his son down on to the floor and stared at her, stupefied. He wore the smell of drink like an overcoat.

'Well,' he said. Ostentatiously he wiped his hands on the seat of his trousers. 'He's not worth hitting.' He looked at the boy on the floor. 'You can get up in safety. I couldn't be bothered knocking you down again.'

There was a sound of a car outside. They all three listened. It stopped outside and the doors slammed. The doctor's footsteps approached the door.

'Well, what is it this time?'

His voice had little patience in it. He stood in the doorway and looked around the room, Maureen's frightened face peering over his shoulder. He took it all in and he sighed.

He knelt down by the woman, his hands felt her body, but he spoke to Minnie.

'Is that you I see there, Minnie MacMahon?'

'Yes.'

'What in the name of God are you doing here in the middle of all this?'

Minnie, exhausted suddenly, moved her hands helplessly. 'I just happened to be passing.'

'At your age you should know better. Come on.' He stood up.

'Me?'

'Of course, child.' He took her by the shoulder and pushed her towards the door. 'I'll bring you home.'

'But . . .'

'But me no buts. Mrs Kelly can wait. She's waited before, and, God knows, she's likely to wait again.'

At the door, he turned: 'Any more trouble out of you this night, Kelly, and I'll have the guards round here, and it won't be one night or two that you'll spend in a cell.'

Mr Kelly muttered something inaudible.

'I'll be back in five minutes. Have some hot water ready for me.'

He shoved Minnie out into the dark and opened the door of the car for her.

The minute she was in, she began to cry. He slammed his door and settled down into his seat. The engine started.

'Don't worry yourself.' They moved off. 'When you're as old as

I am, and you've seen all I've seen of people, you'll learn not to cry. Here.' He handed her a large, clean handkerchief.

'Thanks.'

'She'll recover. It takes more than that to kill a Kelly.' He laughed. A short bark, more it was. 'They always wait till I'm getting into bed.'

They turned in through the gates. The hundred-pound gates, wearily waiting by the side of the road like a couple of people who'd missed a bus and didn't know when the next one would be along. Minnie cried even harder.

'A week or so in hospital and she'll be as right as rain. A good rest for her, in fact. She'll probably lose her baby, but, let's face it, my dear, that'll be no harm.'

He patted her knee. She suddenly noticed there was blood on her hand and wondered if he'd mind her wiping it off with his handkerchief.

'That sounds callous, I know, but it's not. Realistic.'

He stopped at the bottom of the steps. Ivy had left the hall light on for her and it shone through the fanlight, making a pattern on the drive. Home. He leant across her and opened the door.

'You're all done in. Keep out of that kind of mess in future, young lady. Have a good hot drink and a couple of aspirin. It won't seem so bad in the morning.' He pushed her gently out of the car. 'Keep the handkerchief. Regards to your uncle. Haven't caught a sight of him in months. Well, back to the circus.'

His white, disinfected hand flapped out of the window at her as he drove away.

Chapter Six

In spite of the doctor's words about hot drinks and aspirins, things don't at all seem better this morning. Worse, really. For some obscure reason, I feel enormously to blame. The day is like spring, and the sides of the avenue are suddenly covered with crocuses, brilliant yellow and purple. I can see them from where I am sitting. The wind has changed, and blows now in sharp gusts from the lough. Even here, with the window closed, I can smell the salt in the air. If I am to start my garden experiment, I must start at once. Perhaps the spring is what we all need here. The winter seems to have been too long.

*　*　*

The black earth clung to the fork and, heavy, to her boots. As it dried, it patterned her hands with grey. Blisters would form, she knew, at the base of her fingers. It took hard digging to shift the deeply-rooted weeds, and the grey winter-dead grass. The clean patch in front of her seemed minute. She shoved the fork deep into the soil and leant on it. It was one way of keeping warm, anyway. She took off her sweater and threw it over the lichen-covered branch of an apple tree. Branches shot high into the air, long, barren twigs. Same with the peach and pear trees along the wall; black, whippy shoots stretched on and on up, peering over the top of the wall. Useless. Where to begin had been the problem. Why not there? Or there? Just take the fork and turn the soil. And slash. Rake and burn. She blotted her forehead with her sleeve and bent to it again. Four hours' gardening and four hours' writing. That filled the day nicely. Organization. We'd have to see how things came along.

'Having fun?'

Kevin was passing, a sack of potatoes for the kitchen humped on his back.

She became instantly conscious of her damp, purple face, and wiped a muddy hand across it awkwardly. He was going.

'Hey!' He paused and turned slightly back towards her.

'How's your mother?'

'OK.'

'No, but really.'

He swung the sack down on to the ground and took a butt from behind his ear and lit up.

'The doctor took her to the hospital. She'll be OK.'

'And the baby?'

He shrugged. 'Gone.'

'Oh dear.'

'Aren't eight of us enough?' He poked the sack with his toe. 'Perhaps she'll learn some sense now.'

'Sense?'

'And not let him near her any more.' He was silent for a moment. 'He's away.'

'Your father?'

'Ay. He was away off out of the house before the doctor even got back.'

'Where do you think he's gone?'

'I don't know and I don't care. I suppose off with some woman. I only hope he never comes back again.'

'What about the kids?'

'They'll manage.' He fiddled with the top of the sack, uneasy. 'I don't think I'll stay, though.'

'Kevin.'

He shook his head. 'I can't.'

'You promised.'

'I can change my mind.'

Her heart was hammering too hard inside. 'A month, you promised.'

'I can't stay here any longer. If I could only hit him, it would be different, but I can't. It's all talk with me. And you'll never get the money. So, what's the point?'

'I will.'

'I thought I'd go to Dublin and work there for a while. Till I'd made enough to start me off over there.'

'But . . .'

He picked up the sack and stood looking at her. Away beyond him, Ivy shook a rug out of the Major's window. It cracked like a pistol in the wind.

'Will you be going soon?'

'Yes.'

The tolling monotone of the Chapel bell blew towards them. Kevin blessed himself.

'That's twelve.'

'Don't let me keep you.'

'No.'

He walked away from her, weighed down. She bent over the fork again. A drop of water fell on her wrist.

'Rain.' She didn't fool herself.

'Rain,' mumbled Uncle Frank, his fingers groping like a blind man's for the knife and fork. 'Bloody rain, and then black frost. Ruin the hunting. No scent. Horses' legs breaking like matchsticks.'

Tapatapatapa on the cold panes behind her back. Blisters were beginning to form on her hands.

'When I was a young man we had fires in every room and pot flowers from the greenhouse, changed once a week.'

'The winter's nearly over.'

'Ah.'

A tear rolled down his cheek. Minnie wondered if he was really crying, or if his eyes were giving him trouble.

'There'll be next winter.'

She nodded. Her back ached, in spite of a hot bath.

'Things will be different then.'

'Maybe.'

'For sure.'

He laid his knife and fork down neatly on his plate, food untouched. 'I'll be running down to Dublin when the weather gets better. See a few old . . . ah . . . Buy a hunter. Got the boy, you know,' he clicked his fingers in her direction, 'the Kelly boy, to clean up the stables. Ought to get a couple of hunters, if the purse can stand it. Like to be able to mount Bertie if he comes over.'

'Yes.'

'If the purse . . .'

She sighed.

'Got to look up a few . . . mustn't lose touch completely.'

'Quite.'

His foot searched for the bell. They sat in silence until Ivy pushed the door open and came in with her tray.

'Youse are full of bright and lively chitter-chat tonight, I must say. The noise of you near deafened me as I came across the hall.'

She removed the Major's plate from in front of him, and sniffed as she looked at it. 'I might as well go on strike if certain people don't eat the food I put in front of them.'

'A temporary . . .'

'Temporary, my backside. Minnie's my witness. You haven't eaten a square meal since she came home.'

'. . . indisposition.'

'Has he?'

'You must admit I make up for him.'

'Does your uncle know where you went gallivanting off last night?'

Minnie blushed, but didn't speak.

'What's this?'

Ivy clattered dishes on to the tray. 'Away off to the pictures, she was, with Kevin Kelly.'

'Well, so what?'

'None of your lip.'

'With, ah, Kevin Kelly?'

'The very one.'

'I can't see what's so odd about it.'

'He's hardly, ah . . .'

'Ivy, you beastly old goon.'

'. . . a suitable companion.'

'That's it,' said Ivy, 'that's what had to be said. He's hardly a suitable companion, and well you know it.'

'What's unsuitable about him? He's my age. We like chatting to each other, going for walks, or to the movies. What's wrong with that?'

'It's out of the question. What will people say?'

'What people, for heaven's sake? We don't know any people.'

'Your aunt. It's quite out of the . . .'

'Can't take your eyes off her for a moment.'

They both looked terribly old and terribly menacing.

'You're both being impossible.'

'The right place for her is over there.'

'Shut up, Ivy. Just bloody well shut up.'

She jumped to her feet. The Major's hands were shaking so much he had to force them under the edge of the table to keep them still.

'I am amazed. Upset.'

'It's too much of a responsibility for me to be keeping an eye on her the whole time. Suppose something happened.'

'Ivy!'

'Kevin Kelly.'

'Over there. Meeting young people of her own class.'

Minnie laughed, a trifle hysterically. 'Class.'

'Where's your sense? Traipsing round with the son of a tinker.'

'Ha.'

'That's what they all say about her. A tinker's daughter and he put her up the pole and had to marry her. Wouldn't you know it to look at the kids.'

'That gives me and Kevin something else in common, so. Isn't that the sort of thing everyone says about my own mother and father?'

'Minnie!'

'You're upsetting your uncle.'

'How do you know my mother wasn't a tinker, too? You never even bothered to look at her.'

'Minnie.'

His hands clasped and unclasped in terrible distress.

'So don't pull the class angle on me. Maybe I'm finding my own level.'

She slammed out of the room and ran up the stairs.

Ivy scowled at the queen of puddings. Why bother to cook for either of them?

'She's getting the dead spit of her father,' she muttered, more to herself than anyone.

'I think I must just . . .'

He rose with difficulty and made his way to the door. He hesitated for a moment, but didn't turn round, went on across the hall, slowly, and down the passage, the bitch pattering at his heels.

* * *

A faint noise came from downstairs. Minnie turned her head towards the door, a line of light still showed beneath it. The noise again. She raised her head from its warm hollow. I wonder?

'Just people leading their own lives.'

'It must be very late.'

'No need for you to go nosing round.'

Minnie's head slipped down again into the softness of her pillow.

'It's just dawned on me that you want to change the course of the world a little.'

'Doesn't everyone?'

Laughter.

'The poor old world would have a rotten time if that's what everyone was up to. Other people have too much sense. My advice to you is, leave it to the professionals.'

'They don't seem to be doing a very good job.'

'That's not your affair. Relax. You're only young once. Learn to accept things as they are. Slip gracefully from season to season. Living is easy if you don't struggle.'

'So is being eaten by an octopus.'

'You make me tired.'

'Well, you know what you can do.'

'I'm only trying to be helpful.'

'Drop dead.'

'Tttt.'

Heavy eyes, sleep-gritted. The noise again. Slowly she sat up, shaking her head from side to side to shift sleep. What was it? A noise she'd never heard before. Couldn't pin down. Something blowing in the wind? She peered at her watch. Two. The bitch, perhaps? Rot everything.

'Don't say I didn't warn you.'

'Oh, God.'

She slipped her arms into her dressing-gown before getting out of bed. Slippers where? Didn't matter. She opened the door cautiously. It was the hall light that was on, shadowing the wall with giant banisters. Something moved below. She crept to the top of the stairs and peered down over the curving rail. Her uncle lay, face down, on the stairs, a few steps up from the bottom.

'Uncle Frank.'

She ran quickly down and bent over him. The smell. Drink. Drunk, unconscious drunk three steps up from the bottom. Snoring, like a sober man tucked neatly in his bed. She touched his hand. It was ice cold. She shouted up towards the landing.

'You might have informed me of this before. Seeing as how you were being so helpful.'

Bending down, she caught him under the armpits. He groaned pettishly, in his sleep. He seemed to weigh nothing. She pulled him, bumping, up a few stairs. Paused for a breath. He mumbled something that she couldn't catch, and then, with an immense heave, clutching at the banisters, he pulled himself to his feet. She caught at his arm to save him from falling backwards. His eyes opened for a moment and he stared at her. She slung his arm across her shoulder and kept a good hold on his hand. She had him well anchored.

'Up,' she ordered, and together they moved to the next step. He tried to free his hand from her grip.

'Up.'

They moved again.

'I most . . . most strongly . . . I must ob . . .'

'Up.'

'Miss whoever you . . .'

'Up.'

' . . . object.'

'Objection overruled. Up.'

'Ob . . .'

'Up.'

'Miss who . . .'

'I'm Minnie. Again, up. Darling Uncle Proinnseas, don't stop, we were doing so well.'

'Little Minnie.'

'Up.'

Obediently, he moved.

'Little, little Minnie.'

'Getting bigger every day.'

He began to cry. This is the last straw, she thought. Together they heaved up two more steps. Then he stopped and tried to sit down again.

'No. Up. Come on, try again.'

'We mustn't let her know.' His voice was thick and the words hard to catch.

'We won't let anyone know. Come on.'

'Little Minnie. Mustn't let her . . . Let's just keep it a . . .'

'Secret.'

'Just between us two. You and . . .'

'We're nearly there.'

'It's just a temp . . .'

'Do try.'

'Yes.'

They reached the top and slowly crossed the landing to his room. Minnie opened the door.

'A temp . . .'

'Yes.'

He blinked around the room as she switched on the light. His bed was turned back. Dark-blue pyjamas lay folded on the pillows.

'We'll just keep it a secret.'

She pushed him on to the bed and bent to take off his shoes. His weeping turned to foolish giggles.

'It's a long time since any girl put me to bed.'

His hands groped out towards her. Roughly, she pushed them away, and pulled off his coat.

'I'm old.'

'Lie down, now, and get some sleep.'

'Cold all over.'

He was shaking as he fell back on to his neat white pillows. She pulled the clothes up over him. The bed was warm. Ivy had put two bottles in it.

'Old.'

'Sleep.'

She took a handkerchief from her pocket and wiped his sad old eyes, and the tears from his cheeks. His eyes flickered shut and then open again.

'Do we know each other?'

'No. Not one little bit.'

His fingers touched hers. 'Let's promise . . . let's . . .'

'Yes,' she whispered, 'it's all right, we'll keep it a secret.'

'We won't tell Minnie.'

'Don't worry.' She leant over him and kissed his cheek. 'Good night now.'

She closed the door quietly behind her and stood for a moment to see if he would call. She could hear the hall clock ticking in the stillness. She ran like the wind down the stairs and along the passage to the boot-room. She hardly dared open the door. Even the black bitch knew her place. It was a long narrow room. A passage more, leading nowhere. A black leather chair was upright like a sentry, against the end wall. Shelves held saddle soap, brushes, polish, shammies, neatly packed boxes, everything shipshape. Above, in racks, hung the guns, and on the floor, in a long row, stood the boots of fathers and sons for many years back. Even under the single dusty bulb, each move of Minnie's was reflected in their shining convex surfaces. Opposite the door, under the only window, set high up in the wall, was an old shallow sink with a wooden draining board and shining brass taps. The smell was of leather dust and whisky.

Minnie picked up one of the boots. Something moved inside. Cautiously she put her hand into the boot, and her fingers felt the neck of a bottle. She pulled it out. Johnnie Walker, almost empty. She put it down on the floor and tried the next boot. The same, only full. Fourteen bottles she pulled out and set in a row on the flagstones. Fourteen cheery bucks tipped their hats to her. Damn him, anyway, was all she could think; he might at least have gone to hell on Irish. She picked up the first bottle and emptied it down the sink, then slipped dead, smiling Johnnie back in his boot again. And the same, and the same. It was very easy to do. When the last drop was gone, she turned on the taps to wash the lingering oil of whisky down the drain. Then she returned to her bed.

* * *

Vroom.

It was as easy as falling off a log, she thought, staring through Big Jim's lace curtains at the tail end of the Maguires. No wonder people turned to crime in their millions. From the moment the day had begun, it had all been made so easy. She had approached Kevin as he stood in the yard cleaning the Major's car. A fine neat stream of water sprang from the hose in his hand.

'Listen, Kevin.' She came up close beside him and spoke like a conspirator.

'Howaya.'

'Can I have a word with you?'

'Go right ahead.'

He laid the hose on the ground and began rubbing down the car with a grey rag. Water foamed around their feet.

'Not here.'

'Secrets?'

She nodded. He walked across the yard and turned off the tap.

'Where would suit you?'

'We'll just walk down the drive a bit.'

'OK.'

'I just don't want Ivy poking her nose into things.'

'Fair enough.'

Out of the yard and round the corner, a yellow splash of crocuses coloured the bank below the garden wall.

'How are things at home?'

He smiled slightly at her. 'The answer to that's no secret, anyway.'

She blushed. Stopped. Looked down at her fingers, white snakes twining and untwining.

'What I mean is . . . What I really want to ask you . . . would it honestly be an easy job to take those gates down?'

'Oh, girl.'

'Would it?'

'Easiest job in the world. I'd give them a good drop of oil tonight. Ease the hinges. Nothing could be easier.'

'Then there'd be transporting them.'

'I can get the loan of a lorry, anytime.'

'Sure?'

'Positive certain.'

She stared past him at the crocuses for a moment. This was it, then.

'I think we'll have to do it.'

He nodded. Watched her face with care.

'You'll stay, won't you?'

'What made you change your mind?'

'You'll stay?'

'Didn't I say so?'

For a moment their arms were round each other and their cheeks burned together. That was all. She knew, though, by the pounding of his heart against her body, that this was what he wanted, too, and she trembled all over with happiness.

'A deal?'

'Shake on it.'

Solemnly they shook hands.

'I feel far too happy for someone who's just about to start on a life of crime. When'll we do it? Tonight?'

'Hold your horses. We have all sorts of arrangements to make first. I have to get the lorry. You'll have to let the Americans know. Find out where they want the gates delivered. It would be best if I took them up to Dublin. Get them straight out of the district, like, just in case the Major found out they were gone. He probably won't find out for weeks, and then you know nothing.'

'Absolutely nothing.'

'Great girl.' He patted her shoulder abstractedly. 'What's the day?'

'Tuesday.'

'Let's see . . .' His fingers picked at his lower lip as he thought. 'Spin down on your bike and tell them a story. I'll deliver the goods on Thursday wherever they say. And, Minnie.'

'Yes.'

'Cash on the nail. No cheques or promises. Say, no cash no gates.'

'No cash no gates.'

'The very I.T.'

They stared at each other.

'Well, you'd better be getting a move on.'

'Yes.'

'Is your bike pumped up?'

'Oh, yes.'

'Well, then.'

'I'll be going so.'

'You should.'

'Goodbye.'

'Goodbye and good luck.'

'Thanks.'

Vroom. Orange lights flashed and it was gone around the corner.

The boy had been putting the last cases in as she arrived. No one had questioned her story. Mr Maguire had patted her bottom and smiled. He'd always thought the Major would see it his way. People usually did. Mrs Maguire adjusted her curls in the driving mirror and sighed to be away. Not later than noon Thursday at the Shelburne. He'd have made all arrangements. She wiped a smear of lipstick off a front tooth, and withdrew into her mink, like a snail into its shell. Cash, of course. A bellow of laughter nearly choked him. He reckoned nothing would suit the Major like cash in the hand. Her eyes drooped in boredom. He winked at Minnie. Cash in the hand. Works like a magic charm. A disgruntled rattling of bracelets. He winked at Minnie again and slipped into the car beside her. Vroom. Easy as falling off a log.

Big Jim coughed behind her in the darkness.

'Are they away?'

'Just turned the corner.'

'Will you have a cup of tea with me?'

'I can't today, Big Jim, I have to get back.'

'She's going with them.'

'Who?'

'The girl. She'll be off as soon as her papers come.' There was a very long pause. 'She suited me very well.'

'You'll find someone else.'

'I don't doubt.'

'There's something I've been thinking about.'

'Just fire away.'

She sang. From behind the bar, through the kitchen door, the sound came to them. Not a worry on her mind. The New World was at her feet.

'Back there, when you fought the British, you were fighting for freedom, weren't you?'

He scratched his nose. 'That was it. Yes.'

'What I don't understand is, there must have been so many people who didn't know they weren't free. What do you feel when a hero comes along and gives you a present? "Mrs O'Brien, here is your freedom." Do you feel different in any way? Perhaps Mrs O'Brien just continues to worry where the next meal is coming from, or shoes for the children. Aren't those sort of things more important, in fact, than airy-fairy ideas? I get terribly confused.'

'Them old airioplanes is terrible things.'

'Yes.'

'He was the one. I'm too tired these days for answering questions. He asked a power himself in his young days, and I presume he found the answer to some before he died. God rest his soul.'

Gay swansong from the kitchen.

Minnie moved towards the door. The old man's head nodded.

'I'll be going, so. I'll be back sometime soon and we'll have a cup of tea.'

'You never know the minute or the hour. I'll maybe see you and I maybe won't.'

'Of course you will.'

'Please God, child.'

He turned away to peer through the curtains and she skipped out.

'I am becoming a woman of action.' She spoke aloud as the wheels spun.

Laughter.

'And you just leave me alone from now on. There is no longer any need for you to stick around. Go and haunt some other waverer.'

The wheels hummed like an army of bees, and the sun beat warmly on her head. She waved her hand gaily to the rector, who was contemplating a bleak rose bed, secateurs in hand. He raised the secateurs above his head in greeting.

'Your spiritual guide.'

'Oh, hump off.'

'Ah-ah.'

'I'm right. I know I must be right. This exhilaration . . .'

'You had your arms around his unwashed neck and your cheeks burned together, don't think I don't know.'

'I'm tearing up my novel.'

'Quite right, too. Pretentious drivel.'

'Thanks.'

'You're welcome.'

'You just wait and see, we'll do it. He and I. You'll laugh on the other side of your face in a few years, when the garden's paying its way.'

'And then?'

'Wait and see. Perhaps my father was right; we might turn the whole place into a collective . . .'

'Ha ha ha ha. Oh, pardon me if I die laughing.'

'Sneerer.'

'Kid. Fool.'

Whirrr.

Kevin was polishing the car with a chamois. His face was red from stooping. He looked up at her, but continued to polish, his arm circling slowly.

'Well?'

'All fixed.'

He took a deep breath and smiled, enormously. She was thrilled to see the size of the smile. He went on polishing.

'Great.'

'You're really pleased, aren't you?'

'You can say that again. You're a great girl.' He straightened up and took a butt from behind his ear. 'Tell you what I'll do.' He never took his eyes off her. Stuck the butt in his mouth. Flip with a match on his thumbnail and it was alight. He took a deep drag and let the blue smoke float upwards from his mouth. 'While I'm in Dublin, I'll go to a nurseryman and stock up with stuff. Get a bit of expert advice. Open an account, like. We'll swing straight into action. You're a great girl.'

It was like throwing a bone to a dog. She couldn't speak. Ivy's voice shouted from the kitchen.

'That's lunch. I'd better go. I'll see you later.'

'I've things to fix up. I won't be back this afternoon. I'll be below at half eleven tomorrow night with the lorry and some sacking to wrap them in.'

'OK. I'll be there.'

'Minnie.'

'Coming.'

He polished again. Minnie noticed that her uncle's car had never looked so clean.

'Goodbye.'

'Goodbye.'

'Wipe your feet and don't go trekking mud over my clean floor.'

Minnie obediently wiped.

'The Major's not well at all today. There's your dinner on the table. I nearly burst me lungs calling you.'

'I said I was coming.'

'Talking to Master Kevin, no doubt.'

'I went down to the village.'

'It's a pity you never thought to tell me you were going, I've a pile of messages.'

'Sorry.'

Sniff.

'What's the matter with Uncle Frank?'

As if she didn't know. Ivy split open her baked potato and popped a golden ounce of butter into the middle.

'He's not himself at all.'

Oh no? Minnie smiled slightly, but kept her mouth shut.

'The winter doesn't suit him, he's getting on.'

'Ivy, why do you stay?'

'Curiosity killed the cat.'

'Honestly, though. It's a bit grim at times.'

'If you think it's grim, you know what you can do.'

'It's my home. But you don't have to stay.'

'And where would I go? Would you have me working my fingers to the bone for some family I never seen before? I'm too old for that sort of thing.'

Butter dripped from the corner of her mouth. Minnie grinned.

'Or go and live with my niece? No, thanks. Unpaid baby-minder. No life of your own. "Auntie Ivy, would you do this?"; Aunty Ivy, would you ever. I may say I was here before you were ever thought of. Have another potato?'

Minnie shook her head.

'Who'd mind him if I left? I'd like to see some young one, up from the village looking after him the way I do. Haven't I reared you? Been a mother and father to you. And isn't it my duty before

God to keep an eye on you till you're old enough to have a bit of sense for yourself, though you'll break my heart. Now stop asking stupid questions.'

Above their heads, a bell danced on its spring.

'There's the Major. Pop up, like a good girl, and see what he wants. You've young legs.'

'I'd rather not today.'

The bell jangled.

'Patience.' Ivy ran a finger round her gums to unstick the potato flour. 'You'd rather not?'

'Not today.'

'Well, isn't that too bad.'

The bell jangled.

'Off your backside at once and see what's up with him.'

'Ivy . . .'

'Away before I raise my voice.'

Minnie sighed, but got up. She gave a passing kick at the leg of the table, like a small child, and Ivy's tea slopped into her saucer.

'God give me patience.'

'Ivy.'

Minnie closed the door quietly behind her. The heavy curtains were pulled across and only a thin shaft of dusty light came through the crack. The figure in the bed moved and spoke again.

'Ivy.'

'No. It's me.'

'Oh.'

She could see him now, like an old scrag-necked bird in a nest of pillows.

The room was cold.

'Can I do anything for you?'

'No.'

He turned his head from her and a sigh crept out between his lips.

'What did you ring for?'

'I don't remember.'

Exasperation filled her. 'Sure you wouldn't like some Alka Seltzer?'

She crossed the room and pulled back the curtains. The lough was dancing diamonds. The swans bobbed gently just off shore.

'I'm sorry,' she whispered, 'that was terribly rude.'

Hunting trophies, regimental souvenirs, young men, handsome, sleek-haired, the flower of England's youth, smiled from the walls. Almost a laugh came from the bed.

'It's a long time since Alka Seltzer did me any . . .'

She moved over to the end of the bed and stood holding the brass rail with both hands, looking down at him.

'Uncle Proinnseas.'

'The sun is shining.'

'Yes.'

'I like that. I was playing tennis the day war broke out. Sun.'

'About last night.'

'Last night?'

His voice was vague, but she knew he remembered. He closed his eyes and his head lolled.

'You remember.'

He shook his head.

'Don't be silly. If you can remember what you were doing in 1914, you can remember last night.'

'Wired the colonel, and caught the night's mail boat. Memory plays funny tricks.'

The boat trembled under him. The walls creaked. Tollemache and himself, still in their tennis flannels, slim young fingers round the whisky glasses on the polished, heaving bar. Poor old Tollemache, great on the back line, forehand drives skimming the net. Almost unreturnable. He didn't last long. Welsh voices shouting, shore to ship, under the pale lamps, the night grown remarkably cold. Should have changed, the pair of them. Plain youthful exhibitionism not to have changed. Jokes in the mess. Living. 'Sorry, old chap, nothing doing this time.' He felt hot tears. Minnie looked quickly away from his face, stared out of the window at the racing clouds, and gabbled what she had to say.

'I honestly went off my head a little bit last night. I mean, after an episode that you may or may not remember. I . . . er . . . found all your whisky in the boot-room and threw it down the sink. All. I'm sorry. I do realize now that it probably wasn't the right thing to do. I lost my head.'

'Oh,' said the Major. ' "All my little ones, all"?'

'I just thought I'd better tell you.'

'Ah.'

'As you might imagine, it was the first time I've been faced with a . . .'

'. . . situation.'

'Yes. Like that. I lost my head.'

She looked down at him crying in the bed.

'Sure there's nothing I can do?'

'No.' He shook his head.

'Like me to pop down to the village and get you a bottle of whisky?'

'That's the girl,' he whispered, so that Ivy, below in the kitchen, wouldn't hear. 'Johnnie Walker.'

'Just this once, mind you. I'll never do it again.'

'I . . . ah . . . fully appreciate the situation.'

✻   ✻   ✻

It was too bright a night for crime. The moon was full, the trees and ground silver beneath it. Minnie closed the hall door quietly behind her. Her feet, in the silence, exploded on the steps. The granite sparkled. An owl flapped clumsily from one tree to another. The silver sea sighed behind the house, creeping up on the silver shore. The lorry was standing just by the lodge when she arrived. The cab door opened and Kevin jumped down on to the ground, followed by Cormac.

'OK.'

'OK?'

'It should be dead easy. I've given the hinges two doses of oil. Look.'

He went over to one of the gates and pulled it shut. It moved without a murmur. No trouble.

'The pins just lie in the sockets. No screws, or problems of any sort. We should just be able to lift them out and they'll come away.'

She looked at the hinges. It seemed all too simple.

'Think you'll be able to manage?'

'Of course.'

'No point in standing around, then. Let's get on.' He was in a state of remarkable excitement. 'You and Cormac take the outside. I'll go behind. Get a grip wherever you can, and when I say "heave", heave. It'll be heavy, though, mind.'

Cormac whistled a few shrill notes, almost like a secret signal.

'Can't you bloody well shut up?'

Kevin disappeared behind the gate. Minnie and Cormac took up their places and waited for his word.

'Straight and easy,' said Kevin, his voice coming from near the ground. 'OK, then.'

Three pairs of arms strained upwards. The gate quivered. Their fingers were white, like dead fingers, in the moonlight. The palms of Minnie's hands were pools of sweat.

'Relax, relax. If it doesn't move at the first shove, there's no need to go on busting yourselves.'

He had another look at the hinges. His hands must have been sweating, too, Minnie thought, as she watched him wipe them carefully on the back of his trousers.

'Let's have another go.' He went back to his position. 'Right?'

'Right.'

'Heave.'

They heaved, and the gate moved upwards slowly.

'Get a good grip on it,' grunted Kevin, 'or it'll be over on us. I'll try and take the weight if youse'll only steady it.'

Released from its sockets, the weight was a shock that Minnie and Cormac were unprepared for. Frantically they tried to adjust their grip, but the gate slipped slowly and inevitably from their fingers, swaying over backwards into the ditch, with Kevin underneath it.

'Kevin!'

'Get it off me, don't just stand there like a pair of eejits.'

'Are you hurt?'

'Wet. Here, pull the bloody thing. Gently, gently, though; don't go scraping it to bits, it's worth gold.'

She and Cormac half pulled the gate, half lifted it away. Kevin scrambled out of the ditch and wiped the mud off his trousers.

'A couple of men is what you need on a job like this.'

'Well, you haven't got a couple of men, so you'll have to put up with us.'

'As long as you don't kill me the next time. Here, take that end the two of you and let's get it into the lorry.'

They heaved the gate up on to the sacking bed prepared for it, and then Kevin covered it carefully with another layer of sacks.

'Now for number two.'

They got themselves into position. Cormac winked at Minnie

and pulled a face. A black cloud drifted across the moon. They stooped in the sudden darkness, fingers groping.

'Right?'

'Unhunh.'

'Shove.'

The gate came away first push. This time they managed to lower it on to a corner and then gently down on to its side. They were all panting. The cloud drifted on again and the moon silvered the scene. From the village, a bell tolled.

'Midnight,' said Minnie.

'We'd better get this stuck away. Get a grip on it, there. Upsadaisy.'

They lifted it in on top of its partner, and then watched while Kevin tucked more sacking around it. The job was done. Cormac took a butt from his pocket and lit up. Minnie sighed and looked at the lonely gate-posts. Now she felt cold. Kevin lifted the side and tail-board and chained them together. Then they all stood in silence.

'Well,' said Kevin, eventually, 'I'd better get the evidence out of here.' He moved towards the cab.

'You've a case in the cab.'

Kevin avoided Cormac's accusing eyes.

'Everything'll be all right.'

'Yes.'

'No need to worry.'

'No.'

'You've a case in the cab.'

'Of course I've a case in the cab. It's to put the money in.' He looked at Minnie and grinned. 'Suppose he paid me in half-crowns.'

He took something out of his pocket and threw it to his brother. 'Here.'

It was an unopened packet of Gold Flake.

'Get off home, now, and keep your mouth shut. I might see you tomorrow night, but it'll probably be Friday. So long.'

'So long.'

Clutching his cigarettes in one hand, Cormac hurried away round the corner. Kevin opened the door of the cab. Minnie watched. So that's that.

'Once I'm well away, I'll pull up and have a sleep.'

'That sounds very sensible.'

'No point in just flogging on.'

'No.'

'Might fall asleep at the wheel.'

'Yes.'

He let go of the door handle and groped for her hand. His fingers were like ice.

'Will you be OK?'

'Of course.'

'What'll you say, if . . .'

'I don't know. But I'll think of something.'

He nodded, believing her. 'You're honestly a great girl.'

He pulled her against him and awkwardly kissed her cheek. Before she could speak, he was in the cab, door slammed between them. He wound down the window.

'Goodbye.'

He pulled the starter and the engine stuttered.

'Things like petrol?'

'That's all OK. Seen to. Goodbye, again.'

'À bientôt.'

'Who's he, when he's home?'

He backed carefully out between the two posts. A silver hand waved. He was away.

'See you soon,' she answered.

Thursday.

Friday.

Saturday.

The days lay round her neck like a necklace of rocks, weighing her down. Cormac's white face waited round every corner, trying to catch her eye.

On Sunday, church was in the evening. It was almost dark when the Major brought the car round to the front door and blew the horn for her. The evening was mild, and he had discarded his mittens. His discoloured fingers clung to the wheel. He hadn't missed church once since his mother died. They drove in silence all the way. As they approached the gateway, Minnie covered her eyes with a hand. He looked neither to left nor right. His head was bad. She knew what was happening, but refused to believe her own knowledge. The church bell banged. Hurry up. Miss Carton's fingers fluttered on the organ keys. They had no trouble parking, only one other car outside the black wrought-iron gate. The spring grass had started to grow again among the tombstones.

'I will arise and go to my Father . . .'

As the bell stopped, the rector's quiet voice took over. Above, in the rafters, two bats swooped and squeaked.

'Let us pray.'

The congregation of six sank down on to the dusty hassocks. Miss Carton bowed above the keys, hands clasped. Minnie stared at the altar boldly, hands clenched under her chin. She knew. A snake-like draught curled round and round her ankles. The empty pews stirred anxiously. The air smelt of Rentokil and dust. The bats continued their game above the green oil lamps. To leap into the future, to be old and know things. But then, everything, all evidence, pointed to the fact that the old knew very little more than the young. Anyway, she was fussing. There'd been some technical hitch.

'My soul doth magnify the Lord and my spirit doth rejoice . . .'

The Major held the book adjacent to his eyes and his tired voice crackled unharmoniously in the gloom. No point in putting in an appearance if you just stood there with your mouth shut. Hadn't missed a Sunday in years. Keeping some sort of flag flying. God knows what. Never could tell one tune from another. The words were different, embedded since time immemorial in the mind.

'For He that is mighty hath magnified me: and holy is His name. And His mercy is on them that fear Him: throughout all generations.' The Magnificat it was called. The song of the Blessed Virgin Mary. A lovely, bending lady, blue-robed. 'Pray for us sinners now and at the hour of our death.' That was what they said, kneeling in the sweet darkness. The girl from the shop in Baggot Street. The one who killed my grandmother. The Kellys, robbers and drunkards. No. It really will be all right. Ora pro nobis. Intercede for us. Star of the sea. Rose of the world. A sign. What happens when you reach the footstool of God, only to be told you'd taken the wrong turning somewhere along the line? Return to square three. Do not pass Go. Do not collect a hundred pounds. A bat, black leather-geared, swung impudently down towards the altar. The rector, temporarily startled, waved a white hand.

'Lighten our darkness, we beseech Thee.'

A small indication will do, if You care. I can make my way from there. On my own.

'The blessing of God Almighty . . .'

Smiling and nodding to each other, the congregation went out into the dark. They smiled and nodded and shook each other's hands by the overgrown tombstones. The Major clutched at her arm and they walked away together to the car.

Home in silence.

Monday.

The letter came on Tuesday. Across the table, the Major ripped the paper off the Bloodstock Sales Catalogue and dropped it on the floor. He rolled and unrolled the book, until it would lie flat on the table for him, between the teapot and his porridge plate. He had to stoop right down to catch the words. Minnie picked up the blue envelope by her plate. A present from Liverpool; fat, unpractised writing scrawled across the paper. She had never realized that he might write like that. Almost like a child, tongue in teeth. She put her finger under the flap of the envelope and pulled it open. Anger with herself made her hands shake. Almost like Uncle Proinnseas, morning-after blues.

'Dear Minnie . . .'

Her eyes rose above the formal words. No address. Only 'Saturday'. On Saturday she had still thought there must be a technical hitch.

' . . . This, as you can imagine, is a hard letter to write.' (And, oh boy, oh boy, it's not too easy a letter to receive.)

The Major turned a page in his catalogue and cleared his throat.

' . . . I feel very bad, doing this to you. But I had to leave. You saw how things were. It seemed like an opportunity from heaven. Tomorrow I go to Birmingham. A fellow I met on the boat says he can fix me up with a job there. I know you're too good and understanding to set the guards after me. I will be sending you a few pounds each month till the money is paid back. I'm not a criminal. Please don't think too badly of me.'

There were another couple of lines, but she couldn't read them. She folded the letter neatly in four and put it back in the envelope. On the back of the envelope Kevin had written: 'Saint Anthony guide'. That was good for a laugh, anyway.

'Uncle Frank.'

'Ha?' He didn't look up from the catalogue.

'I need your full attention.'

He looked at her grudgingly. 'What is it now?'

'More confessions.'

'I only ask to be left alone.' He rattled the paper on the table irritably.

'The gates.'

Her eyes filled with burning tears. He looked at her, without any comprehension.

'I stole them. Rather, I arranged for them to be stolen. It's absolutely all my fault.'

'What the hell are you talking about?'

'I sold your gates to the Americans — actually, I arranged for them to be sold to the Americans, and now the person who was my . . . accomplice has gone to England with the money.'

She held out her private letter towards him. He waved it away.

'I am completely at sea.'

'I sold your gates.'

'Yes, yes, yes. But might I ask why?'

'I thought if we could get some money we could get the garden on its feet and then gradually . . .'

'I see.'

'. . . rehabilitate.'

'A big word.'

'It was all done with the best intentions.'

'So you stole my gates.'

'I didn't intend to keep any of the . . .'

'And sold them to those appalling Americans. You and your . . . ah . . . accomplice.'

'I thought . . .'

'No doubt you thought that you could turn your precious Ireland into paradise with a hundred pounds.'

'Well, no, but . . .'

'I suppose you thought that you were going to rehabilitate me, too, the night you threw all my whisky down the drain.'

She shook her head. 'That was panic. This time I thought I was doing the right thing.'

'You didn't seem to choose the right accomplice. I suppose I'll have to go to the police.'

She was crying.

'Please, no. I'll pay it all back.'

'If I'd wanted the bloody money, I'd have sold the gates myself. At least they were mine to sell. Wanted, as opposed to needed. My wine merchants' bill alone is a hundred and fifty pounds. They can wait, and make a claim on my estate when I'm gone. What's left of it.'

'He says he'll send the money back, a few pounds a month.'

'And you believe him?'

'Yes.'

'You amaze me.'

There was a long silence. Minnie blew her nose on her napkin. The Major sighed. Then he leant over at last and touched her hand.

'We all want the world to be perfect, and there are moments, luckily brief, in some of our lives when we feel we have to do something about its imperfection. It's ah, inadvisable. Don't worry about other people, they don't worry about you. All my life people have stolen things from me, so your little bit of petty pilfering doesn't surprise me too much. My father stole my career, and thought he was doing me a good turn when he forced me to take over this place. I hate it. I've always hated it. It's gone on from there. There's really not much left for people to take from me any longer. My privacy.'

'I'm sorry.'

He looked longingly at the Bloodstock Sales Catalogue.

'Always was rotten at speechifying. What was it you said the other day you were going to do? Hens, no. Writing a book. That was it.'

He got up slowly.

'Yes.'

He tucked his paper into his pocket.

'I must go. Must be getting on with . . . Why don't you pop upstairs and get on with writing your book, or whatever? Keep you out of mischief.'

He wandered towards the door. 'Things to do. Mustn't waste time talking.'

He turned and looked at her. His eyes had almost forgotten already. 'Spring soon.'

'Yes.'

Her fingers started tearing the thick blue paper across and across. Out in the kitchen Ivy would piece it all together and know. What matter, really.

'When the weather becomes more, ah, clement, we must get about a bit. You're growing up. Must meet some . . .' His young days whirlpooled in his head. 'Young people like a bit of fun from time to time.'

'Yes.'

Inspiration came to him.

'Tennis,' he said, clutching at the door knob. 'We'll get the tennis court into shape. Yes. Must speak to Kelly. Young people . . . when the weather . . . yes.'

He nodded abruptly and opened the door.

'Well. . .'

'See you later.'

'. . . au revoir.'

ISLA DEWAR

Women Talking Dirty

Ellen Quinn kept her sanity in the suffocating Edinburgh suburb where she grew up by imagining it was a seething hotbed of intrigue. A neglected child, she's still looking for love as an adult; and so she finds herself married to Daniel. How could she know that he would misbehave, and that, with all the love and sex she could want, there'd still be something missing?

Cora O'Brien is the total opposite; outrageous and outspoken, she inspires the children she teaches with the same enthusiasm – often to the dismay of their parents. The city can't soften her Highland lilt, but her lifestyle would raise a few eyebrows back home and her mother already thinks she's the wrong sort of woman – the naughty sort. But her vividness is a facade; most of her secrets she's still keeping to herself.

Fast friends from the start, Ellen and Cora may have plenty to learn about life, but they always have vodka and each other to talk to when the unexpected arrives . . .

'Genuinely moving and evocative' *Scotland on Sunday*

'Appealingly spirited . . . for sparkiness, freshness and verve, it's worth reading' *Mail on Sunday*

0 7472 5113 4

review

LILIAN FASCHINGER

Magdalena the Sinner

'Meet Magdalena Leitner, codename "the Sinner".
She is a killer seven times over, clad in a second-
skin, black leather motorcycle suit. She is Austrian
– but not the yodelling type. Rather, she's bent on a
singular, sinister mission: to force her confession
upon the village priest she has kidnapped at
gunpoint . . .

'As she tears through the European Union in search
of love, liberty and in pursuit of happiness,
Magdalena charges at the windmills of bourgeois
mores, Church hypocrisy, nationalist instincts, and
our selfish failure to listen to or care for others . . .
Unfettered by moral scruples or social constraints,
our leather-clad heroine acts out every woman's
most subversive wish – and every man's – as she
roars through conventions on her Puch . . .

'In the end, we, like the priest, are wholly in
Magdalena's spell, and want this magical morality
tale to go on and on and on' Cristina Odone,
Literary Review

'Faschinger rings the changes with wit and
ingenuity . . . Magdalena is a spellbinding raconteur'
Margaret Walters, *The Sunday Times*

0 7472 5459 1

review

*If you enjoyed this book here is a selection of
other bestselling Review titles from Headline*

EX UTERO	Laurie Foos	£6.99 ☐
MAGDALENA THE SINNER	Lilian Faschinger	£6.99 ☐
WOMEN TALKING DIRTY	Isla Dewar	£6.99 ☐
THE RETURN OF JOHN MCNAB	Andrew Grieg	£5.99 ☐
SNOW ON THE MOON	Keith Heller	£6.99 ☐
NEVER FAR FROM NOWHERE	Andrea Levy	£6.99 ☐
LEARNING TO DRIVE	William Norwich	£6.99 ☐
SEX, LIES AND LITIGATION	Tyne O'Connell	£6.99 ☐
THE INNOCENCE OF ROAST CHICKEN	Jo-Anne Richards	£6.99 ☐
DON'T STEP ON THE LINES	Ben Richards	£6.99 ☐
SILENCE OF THE HEART	Elizabeth Latham	£6.99 ☐
A PASSAGE OF LIVES	Tim Waterstone	£6.99 ☐

Headline books are available at your local bookshop or newsagent. Alternatively, books can be ordered direct from the publisher. Just tick the titles you want and fill in the form below. Prices and availability subject to change without notice.

Buy four books from the selection above and get free postage and packaging and delivery within 48 hours. Just send a cheque or postal order made payable to Bookpoint Ltd to the value of the total cover price of the four books. Alternatively, if you wish to buy fewer than four books the following postage and packaging applies:

UK and BFPO £4.30 for one book; £6.30 for two books; £8.30 for three books.

Overseas and Eire: £4.80 for one book; £7.10 for 2 or 3 books (surface mail)

Please enclose a cheque or postal order made payable to *Bookpoint Limited*, and send to: Headline Publishing Ltd, 39 Milton Park, Abingdon, OXON OX14 4TD, UK.
Email Address: orders@bookpoint.co.uk

If you would prefer to pay by credit card, our call team would be delighted to take your order by telephone. Our direct line 01235 400 414 (lines open 9.00 am–6.00 pm Monday to Saturday 24 hour message answering service). Alternatively you can send a fax on 01235 400 454.

Name ....

Address ....

....

....

If you would prefer to pay by credit card, please complete:
Please debit my Visa/Access/Diner's Card/American Express (delete as applicable) card number:

Signature .... Expiry Date..............